Judy Moody & Judy Moody Declares Independence

Megan McDonald grew up in Pennsylvania, USA, the youngest of five girls. All her family were great storytellers, and she claims she couldn't get a word in edgeways, so she began to write her stories down instead. Megan received a BA in Children's Literature and worked in bookshops, libraries and schools before becoming a full-time writer. Megan and her husband, Richard, live in Sebastopol, California, with a dog, two adopted horses and fifteen wild turkeys that like to hang out on the back porch.

Peter Reynolds created and "published" his own newspapers, books and magazines from the age of seven with his twin brother, Paul. He studied art at the Massachusetts College of Art and went on to set up his own successful production company. Peter says that his mission is to "tell stories that matter". He lives in Dedham, Massachusetts, just down the road from his twin brother.

Novels by Megan McDonald:
All the Stars in the Sky: A Dear America Diary
The Bridge to Nowhere
Judy Moody Gets Famous!
Judy Moody Saves the World!
Judy Moody Predicts the Future
Doctor Judy Moody
Stink: The Incredible Shrinking Kid
Shadows in the Glasshouse
The Sisters Club

Picture books by Megan McDonald:
Ant and Honey Bee: What a Pair!
Baya, Baya, Lulla-by-a
Bedbugs
Beetle McGrady Eats Bugs!
The Great Pumpkin Switch
Insects Are My Life
Is This a House for Hermit Crab?
Penguin and Little Blue
The Potato Man
Reptiles Are My Life
Saving the Liberty Bell

Picture books written and illustrated
by Peter H. Reynolds:
The Dot
Ish
The North Star
Sydney's Star

Novels illustrated by Peter H. Reynolds:
Judy Moody Gets Famous!
Judy Moody Saves the World!
Judy Moody Predicts the Future
Doctor Judy Moody
Olivia Kidney by Ellen Potter

Judy Moody & Judy Moody Declares Independence

Megan McDonald

illustrated by
Peter Reynolds

WALKER BOOKS
AND SUBSIDIARIES
LONDON • BOSTON • SYDNEY • AUCKLAND

For my sisters, Susan, Deborah, Michele, Melissa.
In memory of Jon and Mary Louise McDonald
M.M.

For my daughter, Sarah, and her cat, Twinkles.
To Diana Gaikazova, who declared independence
and is making history of her own
P.H.R.

The author extends special thanks to Hailey and Randi Reel.

First published individually by Walker Books Ltd
87 Vauxhall Walk, London SE11 5HJ
as *Judy Moody* (2001)
and *Judy Moody Declares Independence* (2005)

This edition published 2006
2 4 6 8 10 9 7 5 3 1

This book has been typeset in Stone Informal

Printed in Great Britain by J.H. Haynes & Co. Ltd

British Library Cataloguing in Publication Data:
a catalogue record for this book is
available from the British Library

ISBN–13: 978-1-4063-0327-8
ISBN–10: 1-4063-0327-5

www.walkerbooks.co.uk

Judy Moody

Megan McDonald

illustrated by
Peter Reynolds

Table of Contents

Who's Who

Roar!
Star of the show.

Judy's mother.

Judy's father.

Judy's younger brother.

Judy's cat.

Judy's best friend
since FOR EVER.

Judy's friend.

Judy's teacher.

A Bad Mood

Judy Moody did not want to give up summer. She did not feel like brushing her hair every day. She did not feel like memorizing spelling words. And she did not want to sit next to Frank Pearl, who ate paste, in class.

Judy Moody was in a mood.

Not a good mood. A bad mood. A mad-face mood. Even the smell of her new Grouchy pencils could not get her out of bed.

eL SOL
PROTECT t
Vanill
ice crea

JELLY
BEAN

"First day of school!" sang her mother. "Shake a leg and get dressed."

Judy Moody slunk down under the covers and put a pillow over her head.

"Judy? Did you hear me?"

"ROAR!" said Judy.

She would have to get used to a new desk and a new classroom. Her new desk would not have an armadillo sticker with her name on it, like her old one last year. Her new classroom would not have a porcupine named Roger.

And with her luck, she'd get stuck sitting in the first row, where Mr Todd could see every time she tried to pass a note to her best friend, Rocky.

Mum poked her head inside Judy's room

again. "And think about brushing that hair, OK?"

One of the worst things about the first day of school was that everybody came back from summer wearing new T-shirts that said DISNEY WORLD or SEA WORLD or JAMESTOWN: HOME OF POCAHONTAS. Judy searched her top drawer and her bottom drawer and even her underwear drawer. She could not find one shirt with words.

She wore her tiger-striped pyjama pants on the bottom and a plain old no-words T-shirt on top.

"She's wearing pyjamas!" said her brother, Stink, when she came downstairs. "You can't wear pyjamas to school!"

Star FLAKES
S P

Stink thought he knew everything now that he was starting second grade. Judy glared at him with one of her famous troll-eyes stares.

"Judy can change after breakfast," Mum said.

"I made sunny-side-up eggs for the first day of school," said Dad. "There's squishy bread for dipping."

There was nothing sunny about Judy's egg – the yellow middle was broken. Judy slid her wobbly egg into the napkin on her lap and fed it to Mouse, their cat, under the table.

"Summer is over, and I didn't even go anywhere," said Judy.

"You went to Gramma Lou's," said Mum.

"But that was right here in boring old Virginia. And I didn't get to eat hot dogs and ride a roller coaster or see a whale," said Judy.

"You rode a bumper car," said Mum.

"Baby cars. At the mall," Judy said.

"You went fishing and ate shark," said Dad.

"She ate a shark?" asked Stink.

"I ate a shark?" asked Judy.

"Yes," said Dad. "Remember the fish we bought at the market when we couldn't catch any?"

"I ate a shark!" said Judy Moody.

Judy Moody ran back to her room and peeled off her shirt. She took out a fat marker and drew a big-mouthed shark with lots of teeth. I ATE A SHARK, she wrote in capitals.

Judy ran out the door to the bus. She didn't wait for Stink. She didn't wait for kisses from Dad or hugs from Mum. She was in a hurry to show Rocky her new T-shirt with words.

She almost forgot her bad mood until she saw Rocky practising card tricks at the bus stop. He was wearing a giant-sized blue and white T-shirt with fancy letters and a picture of the Loch Ness Monster roller coaster.

"Like my new T-shirt?" he asked. "I got it at Busch Gardens."

"No," said Judy Moody, even though she secretly liked the shirt.

"I like your shark," said Rocky. When Judy didn't say anything, he asked, "Are you in a bad mood or something?"

"Or something," said Judy Moody.

Roar!

When Judy Moody arrived in third grade, her teacher, Mr Todd, stood by the door, welcoming everyone. "Hello there, Judy."

"Hello, Mr Toad," said Judy. She cracked herself up.

"Class, please hang your backpacks on the hooks and put your lunches in the cubbies," said Mr Todd.

Judy Moody looked around the classroom.

"Do you have a porcupine named Roger?" Judy asked Mr Todd.

"No, but we have a turtle named Tucson. Do you like turtles?"

She liked turtles! But she caught herself just in time. "No. I like toads." Judy cracked up again.

"Rocky, your seat is over by the window, and Judy, yours is right up front," said Mr Todd.

"I knew it," said Judy. She surveyed her new front-row desk. It didn't have an armadillo sticker with her name on it.

Guess Who sat across the aisle from her. Frank Eats-Paste Pearl. He glanced at Judy sideways, then bent his thumb all the way back, touching his wrist. Judy

GINO'S EXTRA-CHEESE

rolled her tongue like a hot dog back at him.

"You like sharks too?" he asked, passing her a small white envelope with her name on it.

Ever since they had danced the maypole together in kindergarten, this boy would not leave her alone. In first grade Frank Pearl sent her five valentines. In second grade he gave her a cupcake on Halloween, on Thanksgiving and on Martin Luther King, Jr Day. Now, on the first day of third grade, he gave her a birthday party invitation. Judy checked the date inside – his birthday was not for three weeks! Even a real shark would not scare him off.

"Can I look inside your desk?" asked Judy. He moved to one side. No sign of paste.

Mr Todd stood in front of the class. GINO'S EXTRA-CHEESE PIZZA was printed in large letters on the board.

"Are we having extra-cheese pizza for lunch?" Judy asked.

"For Spelling." Mr Todd held his finger to his lips like it was a secret. "You'll see."

Then he said, "OK! Third grade! Listen up! We're going to try something different to kick off the year, as a way of getting to know one another. This year, each of you will make your own Me collage. All about YOU. You can draw or cut out pictures and paste things to your collage that tell the class what makes you YOU."

A Me collage! It sounded fun to Judy, but she didn't say so.

"We don't have to draw a map of our family, then?" asked Jessica Finch.

"I'm passing out a list of ideas for things you might include, like your family. I'm also giving everyone a folder for collecting the things you want to put on your collage. We'll work on these as we have time over the next month. At the end of September you'll each get a chance to tell the class about YOU."

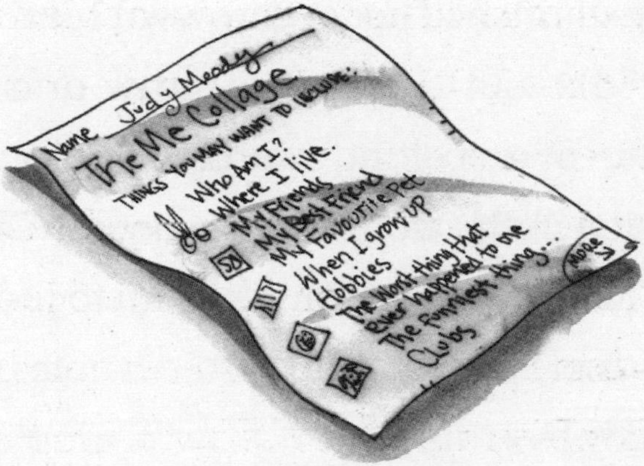

All through Language Arts and Social Studies, Judy thought about one thing – herself. Judy Moody, star of her own Me collage. Maybe third grade wasn't so bad after all.

"OK, everybody. Time for Spelling."

"Yuck. Spelling," Judy said under her breath, remembering her bad mood.

"Yuck. Spelling," Frank Pearl agreed. Judy squinched her eyebrows at him.

"Take out a piece of paper and write down five spelling words you can find hidden in the words on the board: GINO'S EXTRA-CHEESE PIZZA."

"Cool Spelling, huh?" said a note passed to Judy by Frank.

"No," she wrote back on her hand, flashing it at him.

Judy took out her brand-new package of Grouchy pencils with mad faces on them. *GROUCHY pencils – for completely impossible moods,* said the package. *Ever see a pencil that looks like it got up on the wrong side of the bed?*

Perfect. The new Grouchy pencil helped her think. She found the words TREE, TEXAS and TAXI hidden in Mr Todd's spelling on the board. But instead she wrote down (1) NO (2) NO (3) NO (4) NO (5) NO.

"Who would like to tell the class five words they came up with?" asked Mr Todd.

Judy's hand shot up.

"Judy?"

"NO, NO, NO, NO, NO!" said Judy.

"That's one word. I need four more. Come up and write them on the board."

Judy Moody did not write TREE,

TEXAS and TAXI. Instead she wrote RAT and GNAT.

"How about BRAT?" called Rocky.

"There's no *B*," said Frank Pearl.

TIGER, wrote Judy.

"One more word," said Mr Todd.

SPAT, wrote Judy.

"Can you use any of those words in a sentence, Judy?" asked Mr Todd.

"The tiger spat on the rat and the gnat."

The whole class cracked up. Frank laughed so hard he snorted.

"Are you in a bad mood today?" asked Mr Todd.

"ROAR," said Judy Moody.

"That's too bad," said Mr Todd. "I was just about to ask who wants to go down to the office and pick up the pizza. It's a welcome-back surprise."

"Pizza? Pizza! For real?" The room buzzed with excitement.

Judy Moody wanted to be the one to pick up the pizza. She wanted to be the one to open the box. She wanted to be the one who got to keep the little three-legged plastic table that kept the box top from sticking to the pizza.

"So. Who would like to pick up the pizza today?" asked Mr Todd.

"Me!" yelled Judy. "Me! Me! Me! Me! Me!" everyone shouted at once, waving their hands like windmills in the air.

Rocky raised his hand without saying a word.

"Rocky, would you like to pick up the pizza?"

"Sure!" said Rocky.

"Luck-y!" Judy said.

When Rocky came back with the pizza, the class grew quiet, everyone chewing teeny-weeny cheesy squares of Gino's pizza and listening to Mr Todd read them a chapter from a book about a pepperoni pizza-eating dog.

When he finished reading, Judy asked, "Mr Todd, can I look at your little pizza table?"

"That does look like a miniature table, Judy. I never thought of it that way."

"I collect them," said Judy Moody. She didn't really collect them – yet. So far she had collections of twenty-seven dead moths, a handful of old scabs, a dozen fancy toothpicks, hundreds of designer Band-Aids (she needed the box tops), a box of body parts (from dolls!) including three Barbie heads, and four unused erasers shaped like baseballs.

"Tell you what," said Mr Todd. "If you think you can come to third grade in a good mood tomorrow, it's yours. Do you think you can agree to that?"

"Yes, Mr Todd," said Judy. "Yes, yes, yes, yes, YES!"

Two Heads Are Better Than One

Judy was teaching Mouse to walk on two legs when the phone rang.

"Hello?"

All she heard was air.

"Hello?" Judy asked the air.

"Hello, Judy? Are you allowed to come to my party?" a voice asked. A Frank Pearl voice. It had only been two days since he gave her the invitation.

"Wrong number," said Judy, hanging up. She dangled her new pizza table from a string in front of Mouse's nose.

The phone rang again. "Hello? Is this the Moodys'?"

"Not now, Frank. I'm in the middle of an important experiment."

"OK. Bye."

The phone rang a third time.

"The experiment's not over yet," Judy yelled into the phone.

"What experiment?" asked Rocky.

"Never mind," said Judy.

"Let's go to Vic's," said Rocky. "I want to get something for my Me collage." Vic's was the minimart down the hill where they had cool prizes in the jawbreaker machine, like tattoos that washed off and magic tricks.

"Let me ask," said Judy.

"Mum, can I go to Vic's with Rocky?"

"Sure," said Mum.

"Sure!" said Judy, tossing Mouse the pizza table.

"I'm going too," said Stink.

"No, you're not," Judy told him.

"You and Rocky can take him along," said Mum, giving her one of those looks.

"But he doesn't know about crossing through China and Japan on the way," Judy said. Only best friends knew that the first speed bump on the way was crossing into China, the second, Japan.

"I'm sure you could teach him," Mum said.

"Teach me," said Stink.

"Meet me at the manhole," Judy said back into the phone. The manhole was exactly halfway between Judy's front door and Rocky's. Over the summer they had measured it with a very long ball of string.

She ran out the door. Stink ran out the door after her.

Rocky had a dollar. Judy had a dollar. Stink had six pennies.

"If we put our money together, we can buy eight jawbreakers," said Rocky.

"Two heads are better than one," Judy laughed. "Get it?" She unscrunched the dollar bill from her pocket and pointed to George Washington's head.

"I've got six heads," said Stink, showing his pennies.

"That's because you're a monster! Get it?" Judy and Rocky cracked up.

Stink did not have enough money for even one jawbreaker. "You'll break your mouth if you try to eat eight jawbreakers," said Stink. "I could eat at least two for you."

"It's for the prizes," Judy told him.

"Eight quarters give us eight chances to win a magic trick," said Rocky. "I need a new magic trick to paste on my Me collage."

"Hey, wait!" said Judy. "I just remembered – I need my dollar to buy Band-Aids."

"Band-Aids are boring," said Stink. "Besides, you have ten million. Dad says we have more Band-Aids in our bathroom than the Red Cross."

"But I want to be a doctor," said Judy. "Like Elizabeth Blackwell, First Woman Doctor! She started her own hospital. She knew how to operate and put together body parts and everything."

"Body parts. Yuck!" Stink said.

"You saved Band-Aid box tops all summer," said Rocky. "I thought you had enough to send away for that doctor doll."

"I did. I already ordered it. Back in July. I'm still waiting for it to come. But now I need a microscope. You can look at blood or scabs or anything with it!"

Stink asked, "When do we get to China?"

"We're still on Jefferson Street, Stink," Rocky told him.

"Let's look for rocks until we get to China," said Stink.

"Let's see who can find the best one," said Rocky.

The three of them studied the ground as they walked. Judy found five pink pebbles and a Bazooka Joe comic with a fortune

that read: MONEY IS COMING YOUR WAY. Rocky found a blue Lego and a stone with a hole in the middle – a lucky stone!

"I found a black diamond!" said Stink.

"That's just charcoal," said Judy.

"It's just glass," Rocky said.

"Wait!" Judy said, crossing her eyes at Rocky. "I think it's a moon rock! Don't you, Rocky?"

"Yes," said Rocky. "Definitely."

"How do you know?" asked Stink.

"It has craters," Judy said.

"How did it get here?" asked Stink.

"It fell from the sky," said Judy.

"Really?" asked Stink.

"Really," said Rocky. "In my *Space Junk* magazine, it tells how a moon rock fell from space and left a hole in Arizona once."

"And our teacher last year told us how a moon rock hit a dog in Egypt one time. No lie," Judy told her brother. "You're lucky. Moon rocks are billions of years old."

"*Space Junk* says moon rocks are dusty on the outside and sparkly on the inside," said Rocky.

"There's only one way to find out for sure if this is a moon rock then," said Judy. She scouted around for a large rock. Then she clobbered Stink's lump, smashing the moon rock to bits.

"You smashed it!" said Stink.

"Look, I think I see a sparkle!" said Rocky.

"Stink, you found a real moon rock, all right," Judy said.

"It's not a moon rock any more!" cried Stink.

"Look at it this way, Stink," said Judy. "Now you have something better than a moon rock."

"What could be better than a moon rock?" asked Stink.

"Lots and lots of moon dust." Judy and Rocky fell down laughing.

"I'm going home," said Stink. He scraped up handfuls of the smashed rock, filling his pockets with dirt.

Judy and Rocky laughed the rest of the way to China, ran backwards to Japan, then hopped on one foot while patting their heads until they got to Vic's.

At Vic's they put their George Washington heads together for one small box of Band-Aids, and had enough left over for one jawbreaker each. Neither of them won a magic trick for Rocky's Me collage. Not even a troll or a miniature comic book or a tattoo.

"Maybe I could put a jawbreaker on my

collage," said Rocky. "Are you going to stick some Band-Aids on yours?"

"Hey, good idea," said Judy.

"Still a nickel left," Rocky said. So they bought a gumball and saved it for Stink.

When they reached Judy's driveway, Stink ran towards them, his pockets jangling with money. Stink had brown lunch bags lined up on the front steps.

"Guess what!" called Stink. "I made three dollars! Just since I got home."

"No way," said Judy.

"Let's see," said Rocky.

Stink emptied his pockets. Rocky counted twelve quarters.

"What's in the bags?" asked Judy.

"Everybody in the state of Virginia must want it."

"Yeah, what are you selling, anyway?" asked Rocky.

"Moon dust," said Stink.

My Favourite Pet

It was Labor Day, a no-school day. Judy looked up from her Me collage on the dining-room table.

"We need a new pet," Judy announced to her family.

"A new pet? What's wrong with Mouse?" asked Mum. Mouse opened one eye.

"I have to pick MY FAVOURITE PET. How can I pick my favourite when I only have one?"

"Pick Mouse," said Mum.

"Mouse is so old, and she's afraid of everything. Mouse is a lump that purrs."

"You're NOT thinking of a dog, I hope," said Dad. Mouse jumped off the chair and stretched.

"Mouse would definitely not like that," said Judy.

"How about a goldfish?" asked Stink. Mouse rubbed up against Judy's leg.

"Mouse would like that too much," Judy said. "I was thinking of a two-toed sloth."

"Right," said Stink.

"They're neat," said Judy. She showed Stink its picture in her rainforest magazine. "See? They hang upside down all day.

They even sleep upside down."

"You're upside down," said Stink.

"What do they eat?" asked Dad.

"It says here they eat leafcutter ants and fire-bellied toads," Judy read.

"That should be easy," said Stink.

"Tell you what, Judy," said Dad. "Let's take a ride over to the pet store. I'm not saying we'll get a sloth, but it's always fun to look around. Maybe it'll even help me think of a five-letter word for fish that starts with *M* for my crossword puzzle."

"Let's all go," said Mum.

When they arrived at Fur & Fangs, Judy saw snakes and parrots, hermit crabs and guppies. She even saw a five-letter fish word beginning with *M* – a black molly.

"Do you have any two-toed sloths?" she asked the pet store lady.

"Sorry. Fresh out," said the lady.

"How about a newt or a turtle?" asked Dad.

"Did you see the hamsters?" asked Mum.

"Never mind," said Judy. "There's nothing from the rainforest here."

"Maybe they have a stink bug," Stink said.

"One's enough," said Judy, narrowing her eyes at Stink.

They picked out a squeaky toy mouse for Mouse. When they went to pay for it, Judy noticed a green plant with teeth sitting on the counter. "What's that?" she asked the pet store lady.

"A Venus flytrap," the lady said. "It's not

FUR & FANGS
SPECIALS
SNAILS 1.0
SPIDERS 2.00
FLYTRAPS 3.00
MICE 3.50
PARROTS
EDIE
FISH DEPT

an animal, but it doesn't cost much, and it's easy to take care of. See these things that look like mouths with teeth? Each one closes like a trapdoor. It eats bugs around the house. Like flies and ants, that sort of thing. You can feed it a little raw hamburger too."

"Rare," said Judy Moody.

"Cool," said Stink.

"Good idea," said Mum.

"Sold," said Dad.

Judy set her new pet on her desk, where the angle of sunlight hit it just right. Mouse watched from the bottom bunk, with one eye open.

"I can't wait to take my new pet to school

tomorrow for Share and Tell," Judy told Stink. "It's just like a rare plant from the rainforest."

"It is?" Stink asked.

"Sure," said Judy. "Just think. There could be a medicine hiding right here in these funny green teeth. When I'm a doctor,

I'm going to study plants like this and discover cures for ucky diseases."

"What are you going to name it?" asked Stink.

"I don't know yet," said Judy.

"You could call it Bughead, since it likes bugs."

"Nah," said Judy.

Judy watered her new pet. She sprinkled Gro-Fast on the soil. When Stink left, she sang songs to it. "I know an old lady who swallowed a fly..." She sang till the old lady swallowed a horse.

She still couldn't think of a good name. Rumpelstiltskin? Too long. Thing? Maybe.

"Stink!" she called. "Go get me a fly."

"How am I going to catch a fly?" asked Stink.

"One fly. I'll give you a dime."

Stink ran down to the window behind the couch and brought back a fly.

"Gross! That fly is dead."

"It was going to be dead in a minute anyway."

Judy scooped up the dead fly with the tip of her ruler and dropped it into one of the mouths. In a flash the trap closed round the fly. Just like the pet store lady said.

"Rare!" said Judy.

"Snap! Trap!" Stink said, adding sound effects.

"Go get me an ant. A live one this time."

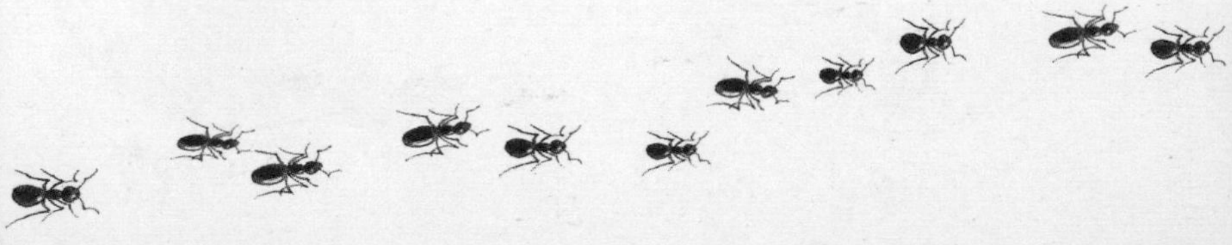

Here's one…

…a real beauty!

Here anty, anty!

No way!

Snap! Trap!

Urp!

Stink wanted to see the Venus flytrap eat again, so he got his sister an ant. "Snap! Trap!" said Judy and Stink when another trap closed.

"Double rare," Judy said. "Stink, go catch me a spider or something."

"I'm tired of catching bugs," said Stink.

"Then go ask Mum or Dad if we have any raw hamburger."

Stink frowned.

"Please, pretty please with bubblegum ice cream on top?" Judy begged. Stink didn't budge. "I'll let you feed it this time."

Stink ran to the kitchen and came back with a hunk of raw hamburger. He plopped a big glob of hamburger into an open trap.

"That's way too much!" Judy yelled, but

it was too late. The mouth snap-trapped round it, hamburger oozing out of its teeth. In a blink the whole arm drooped, collapsing in the dirt.

"You killed it! You're in trouble, Stink. MUM! DAD!" Judy called.

Judy showed her parents what happened. "Stink killed my Venus flytrap!"

"I didn't mean to," said Stink. "The trap closed really fast!"

"It's not dead. It's digesting," said Dad.

"The jaws will probably open by tomorrow morning," said Mum.

"Maybe it's just sleeping or something," said Stink.

"Or something," said Judy.

My Smelly Pet

Tomorrow morning came. The jaws were still closed. Judy tried teasing it with a brand-new ant. "Here you go," she said in her best squeaky baby voice. "You like ants, don't you?" The jaws did not open one tiny centimetre. The plant did not move one trigger hair.

Judy gave up. She carefully lodged the plant in the bottom of her backpack. She'd take it to school, stinky, smelly glob of hamburger and all.

On the bus Judy showed Rocky her new pet. "I couldn't wait to show everybody how it eats. Now it won't even move. And it smells."

"Open sesame!" said Rocky, trying some magic words. Nothing happened.

"Maybe," said Rocky, "the bus will bounce it open."

"Maybe," said Judy. But even the bouncing of the bus did not make her new pet open up.

"If this thing dies, I'm stuck with Mouse for MY FAVOURITE PET," Judy said.

Mr Todd said first thing, "OK, class, take out your Me collage folders. I'll pass around old magazines, and you can spend the next half-hour cutting out pictures for your collages. You still have over three weeks, but I'd like to see how everybody's doing."

Her Me collage folder! Judy had been so busy with her new pet, she had forgotten to bring her folder to school.

Judy Moody sneaked a peek at Frank Pearl's folder. He had cut out pictures of macaroni (favourite food?), ants (favourite pet?) and shoes. Shoes? Frank Pearl's best friend was a pair of shoes?

Judy looked down at the open backpack under her desk. The jaws were still closed. Now her whole backpack was smelly. Judy took the straw from her juice box and poked at the Venus flytrap. No luck. It would never open in time for Share and Tell!

"Well?" Frank asked.

"Well, what?"

"Are you going to come?"

"Where?"

"My birthday party. A week from Saturday. All the boys from our class are coming. And Adrian and Sandy from next door."

Judy Moody did not care if the president himself was coming. She sniffed her backpack. It stunk like a skunk!

"What's in your backpack?" Frank asked.

"None of your beeswax," Judy said.

"It smells like dead tuna fish!" Frank

Pearl said. Judy hoped her Venus flytrap would come back to life and bite Frank Pearl before he ever had another birthday.

Mr Todd came over. "Judy, you haven't cut out any pictures. Do you have your folder?"

"I did – I mean – it was – then – well – no," said Judy. "I got a new pet last night."

"Don't tell me," said Mr Todd. "Your new pet ate your Me collage folder."

"Not exactly. But it did eat one dead fly and one live ant. And then a big glob of—"

"Next time try to remember to bring your folder to school, Judy. And please, everyone, keep homework away from animals!"

"My new pet's not an animal, Mr Todd," Judy said. "And it doesn't eat homework. Just bugs and raw hamburger." She pulled the Venus flytrap from her backpack. Judy could not believe her eyes! Its arm was no longer droopy. The stuck trap was now wide open, and her plant was looking hungry.

"It's MY FAVOURITE PET," said Judy. "Meet Jaws!"

Doctor Judy Moody

Finally! Judy thought the only thing finer in the world than getting Jaws had to be getting a big brown box in the mail with the name DOCTOR JUDY MOODY on it. She was in an operating mood.

"Can I open it?" asked Stink, coming out of his closet fort.

"What does it say right there?" asked Judy, pointing to the label.

"DOCTOR JUDY MOODY," read Stink.

"Exactly," said Judy Moody. "I collected all the box tops."

"I got you some from the school nurse!" said Stink.

"OK. You can go get the scissors."

Stink handed over the scissors. Judy poked through the tape and broke open the brown flaps. Mouse pawed at the sticky tape. Stink's head kept getting in the way.

"Stink! I'm in the middle of an operation!" Judy pulled aside the tissue paper and lifted out the doctor doll.

At last! Judy held the doll in her lap and stroked her silky smooth hair. She made neat little bows in the ties of the doll's blue and white hospital gown. The doll was wearing a hospital bracelet.

"Her name is Hedda-Get-Betta," Judy read.

"Does she do anything?" asked Stink.

"It says here if you turn the knob on top of her head, she gets sick. Then you turn the knob again, and she gets betta. Get it?"

Judy turned the knob on the doll's head until a new face appeared. "She has measles!" said Stink.

"She talks when you hug her too." Judy hugged the doll.

"I have measles," said Hedda-Get-Betta.

Judy turned the knob until another face appeared. Then she hugged the doll again.

"I have chickenpox," said Hedda-Get-Betta.

"Cool," said Stink. "A sick doll. With three heads."

Judy turned the knob once more and hugged the doll. "All better," said Hedda.

"Can I make her get sick, then better?" asked Stink.

"No," said Judy. "I'm the doctor."

Judy opened her doctor kit. "At last I have someone to practise on," she said.

"You practise on me all the time," said Stink.

"Someone who doesn't complain."

"You'd complain too if you had to hold

up a lamp and get bandages all over you. Why can't I ever be Elizabeth Blackwell, First Woman Doctor?"

"For one thing, you're a boy."

"Can I put her arm in a sling?" asked Stink.

"No," said Judy. She held the ear scope up to Hedda's ear and turned on the light.

"Can I mix up some of this blood from your doctor kit?"

"Shh, I'm listening." She held the stethoscope on Hedda. Then she held it on Stink's chest. "Hmm."

"What?" said Stink. "What do you hear?"

"A heartbeat. This can mean only one thing."

"What?"

"You're alive!"

"Can I listen for a heartbeat?"

"OK, OK. But first get me a glass of water to mix the blood in."

"You get it," said Stink.

"Don't touch anything until I get back," said Judy. "Don't even breathe."

As soon as Judy rounded the corner, Stink turned the knob on the doll's head. Measles. He turned the knob again. Chickenpox. Measles. Chickenpox. Measles. Chickenpox. Stink turned Hedda-Get-Betta's head back and forth, over and over, faster and faster.

"Uh-oh," said Stink.

“What?” Judy asked, returning with a sloshing glass of water.

“Her head is stuck,” he said. Judy grabbed Hedda-Get-Betta away from Stink.

“I have chickenpox,” Hedda said. Judy tried to turn the knob. The knob was stuck all right. It would not turn, no matter how hard Judy twisted and yanked and pulled. “I have chickenpox. I have chickenpox,” Hedda said again and again.

“Her head is stuck on chickenpox!” Judy moaned.

“It’s not my fault,” said Stink.

“Is too! Now she’ll never get better!” Judy took Hedda’s pulse. She listened to Hedda’s heart. She checked Hedda’s forehead for a fever. “My first patient, and she’s going to have chickenpox for the rest of her life!"

Judy took the doll to her mother. But Mum could not turn the knob, even with her best opening-pickle-jars twist. Judy took the doll to her father. But Dad could not get the doll's head to turn, even with his best opening-spaghetti-sauce turn.

"What are you going to do?" asked Dad.

"There's only one thing I can think of."

"Give her a shot?" asked Mum.

"No," said Judy. "Band-Aids!"

"Cool!" said Stink.

Stink and Judy put fancy Band-Aids on Hedda-Get-Betta's face, one for every chicken pock. Then they put Band-Aids all over her body. There were Endangered Species Band-Aids, Dinosaurs, Tattoos, Mermaids and Race Cars. Even Glow-in-the-Dark Bloodshot-Eyeball Band-Aids.

"So she won't scratch," said Doctor Judy.

"I'm glad that emergency's over," Dad said.

Judy tried to turn the doll's head one last time. She did not yank or twist or pull. She very slowly, very carefully turned the knob. Hedda's head turned, and her smiling, no-chickenpox face reappeared.

"I cured her!" Judy yelled. She hugged her doll. "All better," said Hedda-Get-Betta.

"Good as new," said Mum and Dad.

"I'm just glad she didn't have spotted fever," said Judy. "I never in a million years would have had enough Band-Aids for that!"

The TP Club

"I think it's going to rain for forty days and forty nights," said Stink.

Judy was hanging blankets from her top bunk to make a rainforest canopy over her bottom bunk. When that was done, she set Jaws on the top bunk for a jungly effect. Who needed a two-toed sloth? She climbed in and spread out her Me collage. Mouse climbed in after her. "Don't get hair on my collage," Judy warned her.

eL SOL
Protect the

Stink stuck his head through the blankets.

"Who's that with hair sticking all out?" he asked, pointing to her collage.

"That's me in a bad mood on the first day of school."

"Where's me? Don't they need to know about brothers?"

"You mean *bothers*?" asked Judy.

She pointed to some dirt glued in the lower left-hand corner.

"I'm dirt?" asked Stink.

Judy cracked up. "That's for selling moon dust," said Judy.

"What's that blob? Blood?"

"Red. MY FAVOURITE COLOUR."

"Are those Spider Web Band-Aids?" Stink asked. "Where'd you get glitter glue? Can I come in there and glitter glue my bat wings?"

Her little brother, the bat freak, was becoming a regular Frank Pearl.

"There's no room, Stink. This is serious. I only have about two more weeks to finish."

Judy cut out a picture of Hedda from the ad in her *Luna Girls* magazine and pasted it in the doctor corner, right next to her drawing of Elizabeth Blackwell copied from an encyclopedia.

She checked Mr Todd's list of collage ideas.

CLUBS. I don't belong to any clubs,

thought Judy. She'd have to skip that one.

HOBBIES. Collecting things was her favourite hobby. But she couldn't paste a scab or a Barbie head to the collage. She taped on the pizza table from her newest collection – the one Mr Todd had given her.

THE WORST THING THAT EVER HAPPENED. She couldn't think of anything. Maybe the worst thing that ever happened to her hadn't happened yet.

THE FUNNIEST THING THAT EVER HAPPENED. When I knocked real spooky on the wall of Stink's room one night and scared him, she thought. But how could she put that on a collage?

Judy puzzled over her Me collage until the rain finally stopped. She called Rocky.

"Meet me at the manhole in five," she told him.

Rocky wore his boa constrictor shirt. Judy wore her boa constrictor shirt. "Same-same!" said Judy and Rocky, slapping hands together twice in a high five, the way they always had when they did something exactly alike.

Judy and Rocky stood on the manhole. "What do you think is under the street?" asked Rocky.

"Oodles and oodles of worms," said Judy.

"Let's collect some in the street and throw them down there," said Rocky.

"Too oogey," said Judy.

"We could look for rainbows in puddles," Rocky suggested.

"Too hard!" said Judy.

"Listen," said Rocky. "I hear toads. We could catch toads!"

Rocky ran back home to get a bucket. When he came back, they cornered a toad and popped the bucket on top of it.

"Gotcha!" Judy held it in her hand. "It feels soft and bumpy. It's kind of cool, but not slimy."

All of a sudden Judy felt something warm and wet in her hand. "Yuck!" she cried. "That toad peed on me." She tossed the toad back into the bucket.

"It's probably just wet from the rain," Rocky said.

"Oh, yeah? Then you pick it up."

Rocky picked up the toad. He held it in

his hand. It felt soft and bumpy and cool-but-not-slimy all at once.

Just then Rocky felt something warm and wet in his hand. "Yuck," Rocky cried. "Now that toad peed on me." He tossed the toad back into the bucket.

"See what I mean?" said Judy. "I can't believe it happened to both of us the same!"

"Same-same!" said Rocky, and they double-high-fived. "Now it's like we're members of the same club. A secret club that only the two of us know about."

"And now we have a club to put on our Me collages," said Judy.

"What should we call it?" asked Rocky.

"The Toad Pee Club!"

"Rare!" said Rocky. "We could put TP

Club on our collages. People will think it stands for the Toilet Paper Club."

"Perfect," Judy said.

"Hey, what are you two doing?" asked Stink, running down the sidewalk in too-big boots.

"Nothing," said Judy, wiping her hands down the sides of her pants.

"Yes, you are," said Stink. "I can tell by your caterpillar eyebrows."

"What caterpillar eyebrows?"

"Your eyebrows make a fuzzy caterpillar when you don't want to tell me something."

Judy Moody never knew she had caterpillar eyebrows before.

"Yeah, a stinging caterpillar," said Judy.

"We're starting a club," said Rocky.

"A secret club," Judy said quickly.

"I like secrets," said Stink. "I want to be in the club."

"You can't just be in the club," said Judy. "Something has to happen to you."

"I want the thing to happen to me too."

"No, you don't," said Judy.

"It's yucky," Rocky said.

"What?" asked Stink.

"Never mind," said Judy.

"You have to pick up that toad," Rocky told Stink.

"This is a trick, isn't it?" asked Stink. "To get me to pick up a slimy, bumpy old toad."

"That's right," said Judy.

Stink picked up the toad anyway. "Hey, it feels … interesting. Like a pickle. I never picked up a toad before," said Stink. "Now can I be in the club?"

"No," said Judy.

"I can't believe it's not slimy," said Stink.

"Just wait," said Rocky.

"I'm not going to get warts or anything, am I?"

"Do you feel anything?" asked Rocky.

"No," said Stink.

"Oh, well," said Judy. "Put the toad back. There. See? You can't be in the club."

Stink started to cry. "But I picked up the toad, and I want to be in the club."

"Don't cry," said Judy. "Trust me, Stink, you don't want to be in this club."

Just then Stink's eyes opened very wide. There was something warm and wet on his hand. Judy Moody and Rocky fell down laughing.

"Am I in the club yet?" asked Stink.

"Yes! Yes! Yes!" said Judy and Rocky. "The Toad Pee Club!"

"Yippee!" cried Stink. "I'm in the Toad Pee Club!"

The Worst Thing Ever

D-day. Doomsday. Dumbday. Saturday. The day of Frank Eats-Paste Pearl's birthday party. I'd rather eat ten jars of paste myself than go to that party, Judy thought.

For three whole weeks she had kept the hand-delivered-by-Frank-Pearl birthday invitation hidden inside the bottom of her Tip-It game, where Mum and Dad (who hated Tip-It) would NEVER find it.

Then today, the very day of the party, it happened. Dad found out.

She, Judy Moody, just had to ask Dad to take her to Fur & Fangs for some toad food. She just happened to be looking at a tadpole kit with real live frog eggs – *Watch tadpoles turn into frogs! See tails shrink, feet grow, legs form!* – hoping to talk Dad into buying it for her when another kit just like it bumped into her. Holding the kit was Frank's mum.

"Judy!" Frank's mum said. "Isn't that funny? It looks like we had the same idea for Frank's present! I thought he'd love watching a tadpole turn into a frog. I was about to buy him the same kit!"

"Um, I wasn't … I mean, you were?"

"Frank's really looking forward to seeing you at his party."

"Party?" Dad's ears perked up. "Whose party?"

"Frank's!" said his mum. "I'm Mrs Pearl, Frank's mum."

"Nice to meet you," said Dad.

"Very nice to meet *you*," said Mrs Pearl. "And Judy, I'll see you this afternoon. Bye for now."

Mrs Pearl put the tadpole kit she was holding back on the shelf.

"Frank LOVES reptiles," she said.

Amphibians, thought Judy.

"Judy, why didn't you just say you needed to come here to get your friend a birthday present? Did I know you had a party to go to today?" Dad asked.

"No."

In the car Judy tried to convince her Dad that there would be kids at the party making rude body noises and calling each other animal-breath names.

"You'll have fun."

"You know, Frank Pearl eats paste," said Judy.

"Look. You've already got the tadpole kit," Dad said.

"I was kind of sort of hoping I could keep it."

"But Mrs Pearl put hers back when she saw yours. At least take it over, Judy."

"Do I have to wrap it?" asked Judy.

From the look on his face, she knew the answer.

Judy Moody wrapped the too-good-for-a-paste-eater present in boring newspaper

(not the comics). Even though the party started at two o'clock, she told Mum and Dad that it didn't start until four o'clock, so she would only have to go for the last disgusting minutes.

The whole family rode in the car to Frank Pearl's house. Even Toady went along, carried by Stink in a yogurt container. Judy held Frank's lumpy present and fell into a bad-mood back-seat slump. Why did Rocky have to go to his grandma's TODAY of all days?

"She's crying!" Stink reported to the front seat.

"Am not!" she said back with her best troll eyes ever.

"Wait here," Judy told her family when they got to Frank's house.

"Go ahead. Have fun," Dad said. "We'll be back for you in half an hour. Forty minutes tops."

"We're only going to the supermarket," said Mum. But they might as well have been going to New Zealand.

Mrs Pearl answered the door. "Judy! We thought you'd changed your mind. C'mon out back. Fra-ank. Judy's here, honey," Mrs Pearl called out to the back-yard.

Judy looked around the yard. All she could see were boys. Boys hurling icing insects at each other and boys mixing chocolate cake with ketchup and boys conducting an experiment with Kool-Aid and a grasshopper.

"Where are the other kids?" asked Judy.

"Everybody's here, honey. Frank's little sister, Maggie, went off to a friend's. I think you know all the boys from school. And there's Adrian and Sandy from next door."

happy birthday

KETCHUP
33

Sandy was a boy. So was Adrian. That Frank Pearl had tricked her – the girls next door were boys! She, Judy Moody, was definitely the one and only girl. Alone. At Frank Pearl's all-boy-except-her birthday party!

Judy wanted to climb right up Frank Pearl's tyre-swing rope and howl like a rainforest monkey. Instead she asked, "Do you have a bathroom?"

Judy decided to stay in the Pearls' bathroom for ever. Or at least until her parents came back from New Zealand. Frank Pearl's all-boy party had to be THE WORST THING THAT EVER HAPPENED to her.

Judy looked for something to do. Uncapping an eyebrow pencil, she drew some sharp new teeth on her faded first-day-of-school shark T-shirt. Rare.

Knock knock.

"Ju-dy? Are you in there?"

Judy turned on the water in a hurry so Mrs Pearl would think she was washing her hands.

"Just a minute!" she called. Water sprayed her all over, soaking her shirt. The sharp new shark teeth blurred and ran.

Judy opened the door. Mrs Pearl said, "Frank was about to open your present, but we couldn't find you."

Back outside, Brad pointed at Judy's wet shirt. "You guys! It's a shark! With black blood dripping from its mouth!"

"Cool!"

"Wow!"

"How'd you do that?"

"Talent," said Judy. "And water."

"Water fight!" Brad took a glass of water and threw it on Adam. Mitchell threw one at Dylan. Frank poured one right over his own head and grinned.

Mrs Pearl whistled, which put a stop to the water battle. "Dylan! Brad! Your parents are here. Don't forget your party favours." Mrs Pearl gave a baby Slinky to each kid as he went out the door. By the time she got to Judy, there were no more baby Slinkies left.

"I must have counted wrong," said Mrs Pearl.

"Or Brad took two," said Frank.

"Here, Judy. I was going to buy these for party favours, but I couldn't find enough." Mrs Pearl handed her a miniature rock and gem collection in a plastic see-through box! Tiny amethyst and jade stones. Even a crackly amber one.

"Thank you, Mrs Pearl!" Judy said, and she meant it. "I love collecting stones and things. Once my brother thought he found a real moon rock!"

"Frank's a collector too," said Mrs Pearl. "All the boys are gone, Frank. Why don't you take Judy up to your room and show her while she waits for her parents?"

"C'mon. Last one up's a rotten banana!" said Frank.

He probably collects paste jars, Judy thought. He probably eats it for a midnight snack.

I get a
KICK
out of
I ATE SHARK

Frank Pearl's shelves were lined with coffee cans and baby food jars. Each one was filled with marbles, rubber bugs, erasers, something. Judy couldn't help asking, "Do you have any baseball erasers?"

"I have ten!" said Frank. "I got them FREE when a real Oriole came to the library."

"Really? Me too!" Judy smiled. She almost said "Same-same" but caught herself just in time.

"I'm taping one to my Me collage, beside my favourite bug, a click beetle, for HOBBIES – you know, collecting things."

"That's my hobby too," Judy told him.

He also had two pencil sharpeners – a Liberty Bell and a brain – and a teeny-tiny flip-book from Vic's. Frank Pearl showed her his buffalo nickel, which he kept in a double-locked piggy bank. "It's not really a collection yet because there's only one."

"That's OK," said Judy.

Frank also had a killer comic book collection, with really old ones like *The Green Hornet*, *Richie Rich*, and *Captain Marvel*. To top it off, he even had a miniature soap collection, with fancy hotel names on the wrappers.

Judy forgot all about wanting to leave. "What's that?" she asked.

"A pitcher plant. It catches insects. They think it's a flower, so they land on it. Then they fall down this tube, and the plant eats them."

"Rare!" said Judy. "I have a Venus flytrap named Jaws."

"I know," said Frank. "That was funny when you brought it to school, how it ate that hamburger and stunk up your backpack and everything."

"Fra-ank! Ju-dy! The Moodys are here."

"I guess I gotta go," Judy told Frank.

"Well, thanks for the tadpole kit," Frank said, twisting a leg of the rubber click beetle from his collection.

"Hey, do you really eat paste?" asked Judy.

"I tasted it one time. For a dare."

"Rare!" Judy said.

Definitely the Worst Thing Ever

Judy's day was off to a grouchy start. This was the day that Stink, her once smelly, sold-dirt-for-moon-dust brother was going with his class to Washington, DC, to see the president's house!

She found out Mum and Dad were going too, as chaperones.

Yours Truly had to stay home and finish her Me collage. She, Judy Moody, still had several bald spots to fill.

"I think my brain has a leak," Judy told her family. "I can't think of one more interesting thing to put on my collage."

Judy sank down on the family-room couch like a balloon that had lost three days' air. "Interesting things could happen to me better in Washington, DC," said Judy.

"You know it's just for the second grade classes, honey," said Mum.

"ROAR!" was all she said.

"We might be home late," Dad told her. "You can go to Rocky's after school. You two can finish up your projects together."

"You'll have fun," said Mum. "And aren't you going to an assembly today for Brush Your Teeth Week?"

How could she forget? One more reason to be grouchy. Stink got to rub elbows with the president while she, Judy Moody, would be shaking the hands of Mr Tooth and Mrs Floss.

Stink waddled into the family room wrapped in a red and white striped tablecloth, looking like he just got hit by a flying picnic.

"What's that?" asked Judy.

"It's a costume for my YOU ARE THE FLAG project. I'm the flag."

"Stink, you're not supposed to *be* the flag. You're supposed to tell what the flag means to you."

"To me it means I *am* the flag."

"What's on your head?"

"A hat. See, each star is a state, like on the flag. There's one for all forty-eight states."

"Guess what. There are fifty states, Stink."

"Nuh-uh. I counted. I crossed them off on my map."

"Count again," Judy said. "You probably forgot Hawaii and Alaska."

"Do you think the president will notice?" asked Stink.

"Stink, the president just about made the states. He'll notice."

"OK, OK. I'll stick two more on."

"Every other second grader writes a flag poem or draws a picture for YOU ARE THE FLAG. *My* brother's a human flag."

"What's wrong with that?"

"You look like a star-spangled mummy and walk like a banana. That's what."

"I get to see a room where everything is made of real gold. Even the curtains and bedspreads. Heather Strong says the lamps are made of diamonds."

"Heather Strong lies," said Judy.

It was no use. She would have to change her Me collage. Frank's birthday party was no longer THE WORST THING EVER. Frank Pearl ate paste for a dare! And he gave her a baby food jar with six ants and a fly for Jaws.

Not meeting the president of her own United fifty States was absolutely and positively THE WORST THING THAT EVER

HAPPENED. Her whole family, including her brother, the human flag, was going to Washington, DC, while she, Judy Moody, would be listening to a talking tooth.

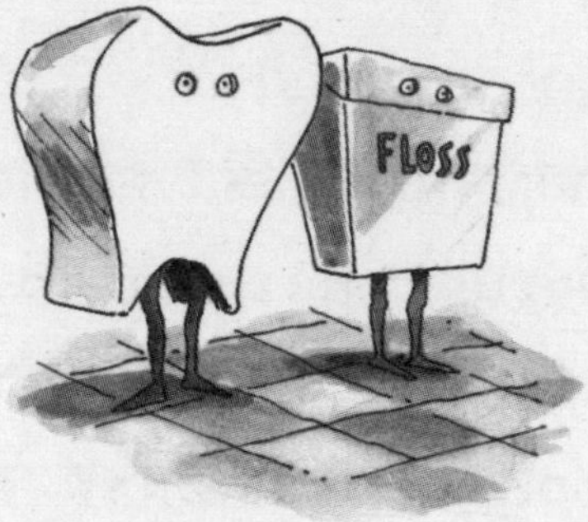

The Funniest Thing Ever

It was pouring outside. Judy's dad would not let her leave for school without an umbrella, and the only one she could find was her first grade yellow ducky one. She wouldn't open a baby umbrella, so she got soaked clear through. The sun is probably shining over the president's house this second, thought Judy. She felt like a bike left out in the rain.

"Frank wants to come over after school too," Rocky told her on the bus. "And I have a brand-new ten-dollar bill from Nay-Nay. We can go to Vic's after school and buy something really rare."

"Do they have any real gold at Vic's?" was all she said.

In Spelling Judy wrote WEASELS when Mr Todd had really said MEASLES. In Science when Jessica Finch threw Judy the ball of yarn for their giant spider web, she dropped it. It rolled out the door just when Ms Tuxedo, the principal, walked past in high heels. And at the Brush Your Teeth Week assembly, Mr Tooth picked Judy to be a cavity. On stage. In front of the whole school.

CAVITY

She could not get her mind off Stink at the president's house, where *she* wasn't. Seeing all that real gold. Would he get to shake the president's hand? Meet the president's daughter? Sit in a gold chair?

"Are flags allowed to talk?" she asked Frank.

"Only if they're talking flags!"

That did it. There would be no living with Stink once he had been to the president's.

On the bus ride home, Rocky squirted Frank with his magic nickel. Frank snorted, wiping the drips on his sleeve. Judy pretended it was funny. Really she was thinking, Stink could be petting the president's puppy right now, this very instant. When Rocky said, "I can't wait to go to Vic's," Judy grunted.

The three of them half ran through leftover puddles all the way to Vic's. Rocky didn't even stop to cross through China and Japan the right way. "What's the big hurry?" she asked.

"I need something," said Rocky, "but there's only one left, and I want to make sure I get it!" he said. When they got to Vic's, Rocky went straight to the counter.

"Over here," Rocky told them. "There's still one left!"

Judy stood on tiptoe to look in a box on top of the counter. Lying in the bottom was ... a hand. A person's hand! Judy almost screamed. Frank almost screamed too. Then they realized it was made out of rubber.

"What do you think?" asked Rocky.

"Rare," said Judy.

"Ace," said Frank. "It looks so real. Fingernails and everything!"

Rocky bought the hand and three fireballs.

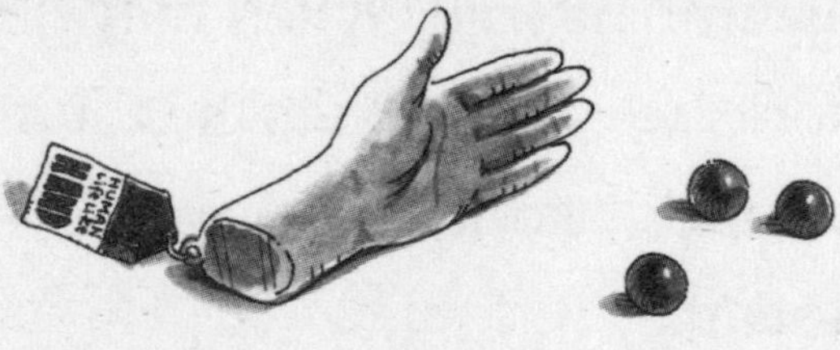

"What are you going to do with your hand?" Frank asked.

"I don't know," said Rocky. "I just like it."

When they got to Rocky's house, Judy tried to work on her Me collage. But she was not in a FUNNIEST THING EVER mood. All the funny stuff that had ever happened to her seemed to have got up and left. Marched right out of her brain like a line of ants from a picnic.

Rocky showed Judy and Frank his finished collage.

"Here's Thomas Jefferson in the window of my house for WHERE I LIVE. I cut him out of play money."

"That's good!" said Frank. "For Jefferson Street."

"The piece of cloth is part of my sling from when I broke my arm, THE WORST

THING EVER. And here's a toilet paper roll for the TP Club, a secret club I'm in," Rocky said, glancing at Judy.

"What kind of club has toilet paper?" asked Frank.

"If I tell you, it won't be a secret."

"Who's this?" Frank asked Rocky, pointing to a lizard.

"Houdini, MY FAVOURITE PET."

"And who's that guy, walking through a brick wall?" Frank asked.

"That's my favourite part. My mum made a copy of a picture of the real Harry Houdini from a library book."

Judy touched a clump of garlic. "Are you trying to scare away vampires or something?"

"That's from one time when I ate a whole thing of garlic by mistake. THE FUNNIEST THING EVER was that I stunk like a skunk for a week!"

"Like Jaws when it ate that hamburger!" said Frank.

"Like Stink when he takes his smelly shoes off," said Judy.

"Is this you?" Frank asked.

"That's me in my magician hat, making a fishbowl disappear."

"Too bad you can't make Stink disappear," said Judy.

"Too bad I'm done," said Rocky. "It would have been really funny to put the rubber hand on my collage."

That's when it happened. An idea. The funniest of all funnies. It orbited Judy's head and landed like a spaceship, the way good ideas do.

"Rocky! You're a genius! Let's go to my

house," Judy said. "And bring the hand."

"You're *not* a genius," said Rocky. "Nobody's home at your house. We could get into all kinds of trouble."

"Exactly!" said Judy. "C'mon. There's a key hidden in the gutter pipe."

"Did you forget something?" asked Frank.

"Yes," Judy said. "I forgot to play a trick on Stink!"

Once inside, Judy raced around her house, looking for the perfect spot to leave the hand, a place where Stink would be sure to find it right away. The couch? Toady's aquarium? The refrigerator? Under his pillow?

The bathroom!

Where?.

Here?

How about here?

Hmm...

Or here?

Maybe here?

I've got it!

Perfect!

In the downstairs bathroom Judy lifted up the toilet seat, just a crack, and perched the hand there, its fingernails hanging over the edge. "It looks real," said Rocky.

"This will scare the president right out of him," said Judy. "For sure."

Back at Rocky's, Judy, Frank and Rocky knelt on Rocky's bed, looking out the window. Every time a car zoomed by on Jefferson Street, they yelled, "It's them!" Finally Judy saw a blue van for real. "Run!" she yelled. "They're pulling into the driveway!"

Stink was so excited telling Judy, Rocky and Frank all about the president's house that Hawaii and Alaska fell off his hat.

Why doesn't he go to the bathroom? thought Judy.

"There's a movie theatre – I swear! Inside the president's house. And a room with a secret door. No lie. Even a clock that tells you when it's time to take a bath," said Stink.

"Rare!" said Judy. "You need one of those."

Go into the bathroom, Stink, she wished silently. As if he had heard, Stink stopped his story. Balancing his hat on his head, he walked into the bathroom and shut the door behind him. The lock clicked.

Mum and Dad asked Judy about the Mr Tooth assembly, but her ears were tuned to the bathroom.

"AAAAAHHHHH!" screamed Stink. He burst out of the bathroom, hat crashing to the floor, stars flying.

"Hey! Dad! Mum! There's somebody in the toilet!"

Judy Moody, Rocky and Frank Pearl fell on the floor laughing.

The Me Collage

Stink watched Judy finish her collage after school the next day. "Almost done," said Judy. "It's due tomorrow."

Stink pointed. "You still have a bald spot right there next to the picture of Jaws."

Judy carefully taped a doll hand from her collection over the empty space. "Not any more," she said.

"That hand? Is it for the trick you played on me?" asked Stink.

"Yes. It's THE FUNNIEST THING EVER," said Judy with a grin.

"You mean you're going to tell your whole class I thought there was somebody in our toilet?"

"Stink, I'm making you famous."

"Couldn't you change my name or something?" asked Stink.

"Or something," said Judy.

When Judy got up the next morning, it was pouring rain again. Something told her to get ready for a bad-mood Friday.

"Let's put your Me collage in a garbage bag so it won't get wet," Dad suggested when she brought it downstairs.

"Dad, I'm not carrying my Me collage in a garbage bag."

ME
JUDY MOODY

"Why not?"

"Did Van Gogh put his *Starry Night* in a garbage bag?"

"She's got a point there," said Mum.

"Garbage bags probably hadn't been invented yet," said Dad. "If Van Gogh had garbage bags, believe me, he would have been smart enough to use them."

"Honey, why don't you take the bus, and Dad'll bring your collage to school after he takes Stink to the dentist?" Mum said. "Stink's taking Toady to school today, so Dad has to drop him off anyway."

"I want to take my collage to school myself. That way I can be sure nothing will happen to it."

"What could happen to it?" asked Mum.

"There could be a tornado," said Stink, "and the wind could make you drop it, and it could get run over by a bus."

"Hardee-har-har," said Judy.

"You do have a lot of other stuff to carry," said her dad. Judy had her lunch, her dad's lab coat so she could dress like a doctor for her talk, Hedda-Get-Betta, her doctor kit and plenty of Band-Aids.

"OK," she said, "but don't squish anything and don't get it wet and it has to be there by eleven o'clock and don't let Stink do *anything.*" She gave her brother her best troll-eyes stare.

"We'll be careful," said Dad.

Judy rode the bus with Rocky, who

practised his squirting nickel magic trick on her for the one hundredth time.

"OK! It works!" Judy told him, wiping drips from her face. Rocky cracked up.

All morning Judy imagined things happening to her collage. What if it fell into a puddle when her father opened the car door? What if Toady got out of Stink's pocket and peed on the collage? What if a tornado came, like Stink said...

Eleven o'clock came, and her collage still was not there. No sign of Stink. Or Dad.

Judy could hardly listen to the other kids showing their Me collages. She kept her eyes glued to the door of 3T.

"Judy, would you like to go next?" asked Mr Todd, startling her.

"I'd like to go last," said Judy.

"Frank?"

"I'd like to go last too," said Frank. "After Judy."

Judy looked at Frank's desk. "Where's your Me collage?" she asked him.

"I didn't bring it. I mean, I'm not finished. I still don't have a CLUB," Frank whispered. "Where's yours?"

"My brother's supposed to bring it," said Judy. She glanced at the door again. There he was! Stink motioned for her to come out in the hall.

Stink looked sick. "What's wrong?" Judy asked.

"If I tell you," said Stink, "you'll be in the worst mood ever."

"Where is it?" asked Judy. "Did you drop my collage in a puddle? Did Toady pee on it?"

"No," said Stink. "Not that."

"Where is it?" she asked again.

"Dad's in the boys' room. Drying it off."

Judy ran down to the boys' room, pushed the door open and went right in. Crumpled paper towels were everywhere. "Dad!"

"Judy!"

"Is it ruined? Let me see!"

Dad held up her collage. Right smack dab in the centre was a big purple stain the size of a pancake. Not a silver dollar one either. A giant, jaggedy triangle – a grape-coloured lake floating in the middle of her collage!

"What happened?" Judy yelled.

"I was drinking Jungle Juice from a box," said Stink, standing behind her in the doorway, "and trying this thing with my straw... I'm sorry."

"Stink! You wrecked it. Dad! How could you let him drink Jungle Juice in the car?"

"Look, it's not that bad," he said. "It almost looks like it's supposed to be there. I'll speak with Mr Todd. Maybe he'll let you have the weekend and we can fix it. Cover it up somehow."

"Maybe we can erase it," said Stink. "With a giant eraser."

"Let me see." Judy held up the collage, looking it over. Even with the purple stain, she could still see the rainforest with Doctor

Judy Moody in the very middle. And none of the Band-Aids had come off.

"Never mind," said Judy.

"Never mind?" asked Dad.

"It's OK," she said. "At least it didn't get run over by a bus in a tornado."

"It's OK?" asked Stink. "You mean you're not going to put a rubber foot in my bed or anything?"

"No," said Judy. She grinned at her brother. "But that is a good idea."

"Look, honey. I know you worked for ever on this. We'll make it up to you somehow."

"I know what to do. Stink, let me have your black marker."

They all went out into the hall, and Stink

dug a marker out of his backpack. Judy set the collage on the floor and drew a black outline round the big purple triangle.

"Are you cuckoo?" asked Stink. "That's just going to make it stand out more."

"That's what I want," said Judy. "Then it'll look like it was supposed to be there all the time."

"I'm proud of you, Judy," said Dad. "The

way you took an accident like this and turned it into something good."

"What's it supposed to be?" Stink asked.

"Virginia," she said. "The state of Pocahontas and Thomas Jefferson. The place WHERE I LIVE."

Band-Aids and Ice Cream

When Judy got back to class, she put on her doctor coat, walked to the front of the room and held her Me collage high. She stood tall, as if her brother had not nearly ruined her masterpiece with Jungle Juice. She tried to look like a person who would grow up to be a doctor and make the world a better place. A person who could turn a bad mood right around.

Judy told about herself and her family, including the time Stink sold moon dust, which explained why her brother was a piece of dirt. She traced the outline of Virginia with her finger to show where she lived. She talked about Rocky, her best friend, and Frank, her new friend. She pointed to a paste jar lid taped to a corner and told the class that Frank ate paste for a dare once.

"Is that Jaws?" asked Brad. "The thing that eats bugs?"

"Yes," said Judy. "Even though I have a cat, Jaws is MY FAVOURITE PET. When I grow up and become a doctor, I want to move to the rainforest and search for medicines in rare plants that could cure ucky diseases."

Judy pointed out the pizza table from Mr Todd and other stuff she collected for HOBBIES. She told the class that she was a member of the TP Club, but that she couldn't tell them what TP stood for.

"This is a picture my parents took of Stink, standing outside the White House in his flag costume." And she explained why it was THE WORST THING THAT EVER HAPPENED to her. Everybody's favourite part of her collage was when she showed the doll hand, coming out of a magazine toilet. So Judy told them about how the worst thing ever turned

Me
JUD
JM
J.M. by J.M.
Who I am
I ate a shark
My favourite pet
JAWS
FUNNIEST THING EVER!
ACME TOILET
RAINFOREST KRUNCH
Where I
Dad
Mum
when I grow up
FRIENDS
ROCKS
STINK

MOODY!
Special offer
HEDDA-GET-BET
Elizabeth Blackwell 1st Woman Doctor
by JM
hobby
When I grow up
Red! My favourite colour
* Pizza Table Collection
TREE BARK
TP CLUB
CLUBS I belong to
Mouse our family pet
House
Frank
STINK
The Worst thing that ever happened
* by JUDY MOODY
MR TODD'S CLASS

into THE FUNNIEST THING EVER.

"Any questions?" she asked the class.

"Who's the old lady?" asked Frank.

Judy explained about Elizabeth Blackwell, First Woman Doctor, and then gave a demonstration of her doctor skills. She put Rocky's arm in a sling and wrapped bandages round Frank's knee. She pulled out her pretend blood, and used Hedda-Get-Betta to show how to apply Band-Aids.

"That's it. Me. Judy Moody."

"Great job, Judy," said Mr Todd. "Class, any comments?"

"I like how you painted Virginia in the middle of your collage to show where you live," said Jessica Finch, "instead of just

using a picture of your house."

"Those Tattoo Band-Aids are the coolest," said Dylan. "I have a blister. Can I have one?"

"I have a hangnail!"

"I have a paper cut!"

"I have a mosquito bite!"

Before Judy knew it, everybody in the whole class was wearing Tattoo Band-Aids.

"Judy Moody, you're a mover and a shaker," said Mr Todd.

"I am?" asked Judy. "What's that mean?"

Mr Todd laughed. "Let's just say it means you have imagination."

What had almost become a bad-mood

Friday had turned into one very fine day. And it wasn't over yet.

When she walked out to get the bus that afternoon, Mum and Dad were waiting to take Judy and Stink for ice cream at Screamin' Mimi's.

"I'm getting that blue ice cream, Rainforest Mist. Like you guys always do!" Stink jumped up and down, holding his pocket with the toad.

"Did your teacher like Toady?" Judy asked.

"Yes, but she was almost in the Toad Pee Club," said Stink. Judy cracked up.

"Mum, Dad, can I ask Rocky and Frank to come too?"

"That's a great idea," Mum said.

Outside Screamin' Mimi's, Judy licked her Rainforest Mist scoop on top of Chocolate Mud, her favourite. She was in her best Judy Moody mood ever.

Stink took Toady out of his pocket and set him on the picnic table. Toady hopped towards a blue drip from Rocky's ice cream cone.

"Toady likes Rainforest Mist!" said Rocky.

"Hey, Frank," Judy asked, "when are you going to finish your Me collage?"

"Mr Todd said I could bring it on Monday."

"You're not done yet?" asked Rocky.

"I *still* don't have anything for CLUBS. The dictionary says a club is three or more people."

SCREAMIN' MiMi'S

Judy looked at Rocky. Rocky looked at Stink. Stink looked at Judy. All three of them looked at Frank.

"If you pick up Toady right now, you can be in a club," said Judy.

"Really?" asked Frank.

"Really and truly," said Judy and Rocky at the same time.

Frank crinkled his nose. "I don't get it."

Rocky laughed. "You will."

Frank scooped up Toady with one hand.

"Use both hands," said Judy.

"Like this," said Rocky, cupping his hands.

"Just hold him a minute," said Stink.

"I still don't get it," said Frank.

"Oh, you'll *get* it," said Judy, Rocky and Stink.

A second later Frank felt something warm and wet in his hand. He crossed his eyes, and they all fell down laughing.

Judy Moody Declares Independence

Megan McDonald

illustrated by
Peter H. Reynolds

BOSTON

Table of Contents

Who's

Judy Moody

Judy Moodington

Dad

Richard John-Hancock Moody

Mum

Kate Betsy-Ross Moody

John Hancock

Fancy First Signer
of the Declaration of
Independence

Tori

Not a Tory; fab collector
of sugar packets

Who

Sybil Ludington

Sybil La-Dee-Da,
Girl Paul Revere

Paul Revere

Bellringer,
false teeth maker,
midnight rider

Stink

Town crier, fond
of musical toilets

Partners in Crime:
The Boston Tub Party

Frank

Rocky

Bean Town, MOO-sa-chu-setts

HEAR YE! HEAR YE!

She, Judy Moody, was in Boston! Bean Town! As in Mas-sa-chu-setts. As in the Cradle of Liberty, Birthplace of Ben Famous Franklin and Paul Revere. Land of the Boston Tea Party and the Declaration of Independence.

"Boston rules," said Judy.

Three best things about Boston so far were:

1. *Freedom from two whole days of school (including one spelling test, two nights of homework and a three-page book report)*
2. *Freedom from riding in the car next to Stink for ten million hours*
3. *Freedom from brushing hair every day*

She, Judy Moody, Rider of the First Subway in America, was finally on her way to the real-and-actual Freedom Trail! The place where her country started. Where it all began.

The American Revolution! The Declaration of Independence! Freedom!

R A R E!

Judy and her family climbed up the stairs and out into the fresh air, heading for the information booth on Boston Common, where Dad bought a guide to the Freedom Trail.

"Did you know there used to be cows right here in this park?" asked Stink. "It says so on that sign."

"Welcome to MOO-sa-chu-setts!" announced Judy. She cracked herself up. If Rocky or Frank Pearl were here, they'd crack up, too.

"Just think," Judy told Stink. "Right now, this very minute, while I am about to follow in the footsteps of freedom, Mr Todd is probably giving Class 3T a spelling test

INFO
H
S
Boston Pops
BOSTON
Boston Red Sox

back in Virginia. Nineteen number-two pencil erasers are being chewed right this very second."

"You're lucky. I had to miss Backwards Shirt Day today."

"The trail starts right here at Boston Common," Dad said.

"Can we go and look at ducks?" asked Stink. "Or frogs? On the map there's a frog pond."

"Stink, we're going on the *Freedom* Trail. Not the *Frog* Trail."

"What should we do first?" asked Mum.

"Tea Party! Boston Tea Party Ship!" said Judy, jumping up and down.

"We came all the way to Boston for a *tea party*?" asked Stink.

"Not that kind of tea party," Mum said.

"The people here first came over from England," said Dad, "because they wanted to have freedom from the king telling them what to do."

"Dad, is this another LBS? Long Boring Story?" asked Stink.

"It's way NOT boring, Stink," said Judy. "It's the beginning of our whole country. This wouldn't even be America if it weren't for this giant tea party they had. See, the Americans wouldn't drink tea from over there in England. No way."

"Not just tea," said Mum. "The British made them pay unfair taxes on lots of things, like stamps and sugar. They called it the Stamp Act and the Sugar Act. But the

Americans didn't have any say about what all the tax money would be used for."

"I don't get it," said Stink.

"We didn't want some grumpy old king to be boss of us," said Judy.

"America wanted to be grown-up and independent," said Mum. "Free from England. Free to make up its own rules and laws."

"So Thomas Jefferson wrote the Declaration of Independence," said Dad.

"And a lot of important people signed it real fancy," said Judy, "like John Hancock, First Signer of the Declaration. Right, Mum?"

"Right," said Mum.

"Before we hit the Freedom Trail, let's go

and see the Liberty Tree," said Dad. "That's where people stood to make important speeches about freedom."

"Like a town crier?" asked Judy.

"That's right," said Dad. "Here we are."

"I don't see any tree," said Stink. "All I see is some old sign on some old building."

"The British cut it down," Dad said. "But that didn't stop the Americans. They just called it the Liberty Stump and kept right on making speeches."

"I don't see any tree stump," said Stink.

"Hello! Use your imagination, Stink," said Judy.

"Kids, stand together in front of the sign so Dad can take your picture."

"I still don't see what's so big about the American Revolution," mumbled Stink.

"Some of us like the American Revolution, Stink," said Judy. "Let freedom ring!" she shouted. Hair flew across her face.

"Judy, I thought I asked you to use a brush this morning," Mum said.

"I did use it," said Judy. "On that pink fuzzy pillow in our hotel room!" Mum poked at Judy's hair, trying to smooth out the bumps. Judy squeezed her eyes shut, making an Ouch Face. Dad snapped the picture.

"Hear ye! Hear ye!" called Judy. "I, Judy Moody, hereby declare freedom from brushing my hair!"

"Then I declare it from brushing my teeth!" said Stink.

"P.U.," said Judy, squinching up her nose.

Dad snapped another picture.

Three worst things about Boston so far were:

1. *Stink*
2. *Stink*
3. *Stink*

The Freedom (from Stink) Trail

"Time to hit the Freedom Trail!" said Dad.

"Let's head up Park Street," Mum said, pointing to a line of red bricks in the pavement. "Follow the red brick road!"

"Look!" Judy cried, running up the hill. "Look at that big fancy gold dome!"

"That's the State House," said Mum, "where the governor works."

"Judy!" Dad called. "No running ahead. Stick close to us."

"Aw," said Judy. "No fair. This is supposed to be the *Freedom* Trail."

"Stay where Dad and I can keep an eye on you," said Mum.

"Roar!" said Judy.

After the State House, Mum and Dad led them to Park Street Church, where the song "My Country 'Tis of Thee" was sung for the very first time.

Stink looked for famous-people initials carved into a tree outside. PLOP! Something hit Stink on the head. "YEE-UCK! Bird poo!" said Stink. Judy cracked up. Mum wiped it off with a tissue.

Stink sang: *"My country pooed on me*
Right near the Pigeon Tree.
Of thee I sing..."

"Mum! Dad!" said Judy, covering her ears. "Make him stop!"

Judy ran ahead. "Hurry up, you guys! The church has an old graveyard!"

Mum stopped to read the plaque on the gate at the entrance: "'May the youth of today ... be inspired with the patriotism of Paul Revere.'"

"Paul Revere's grave is here!" Judy shouted. "So is John Hancock's, First Signer of the Declaration. For real!"

Judy saw gravestones with angel wings, skulls and bones, and a giant hand with one finger pointing to the sky.

"'Here lies buried Samuel Adams, Signer of the Declaration of Independence,'" Dad read. "Did you know he also gave the secret signal at the Boston Tea Party?"

"'Here lyes y body of Mary Goose,'" Stink read. "Boy, they sure did spell funny."

"And I thought I was the world's worst speller," said Judy. She took out pencil and paper from her backpack and made a rubbing of Mother Goose's grave. Stink made a rubbing of a skull and bones, a leaf and a crack in the pavement.

"Do we have to keep seeing stuff?" Stink asked when they got to the Ben Franklin statue. "So far it's just a bunch of dead guys and some old stuff that isn't even there any more."

BOSTON RED SOX

"But what about the Boston Tea Party?" asked Judy.

"AW!" Stink whined. "I have to go to the toilet."

"Stink, don't be the town crier," said Judy. "I mean, the town *crybaby*!"

"Tell you what," said Mum. "Dad, why don't you and Judy go and see the Paul Revere House? I'll take Stink to the toilet, and we'll meet back here."

"Great idea!" said Dad.

Judy and Dad walked and walked. At last they came to 19 North Square. "Did you know that Paul Revere made false teeth?" Dad asked. "And he made the first bells in America. He even drew cartoons."

THE PAUL REVERE HOUSE

"Wow!" said Judy. "All that on top of riding his horse lightning-fast and warning everybody that the British were coming!"

"That's right," Dad said. "A friend of Paul Revere's climbed out of a window and over a rooftop to give the lantern signal from the Old North Church: one if by land, two if by sea..."

"Star-spangled bananas!" said Judy.

"And it says here he rode all the way to Philadelphia to tell them the news about the Boston Tea Party," Dad said.

"Tea party? Did somebody say *tea party*?" asked Judy.

"OK, OK. Let's head back to meet Mum and Stink."

Judy ran up to Stink. "You missed it, Stink!" She told him all about the guy climbing out of the window and giving the secret signal.

"Who cares?" said Stink. "We saw something better!"

"What?" said Judy. "A two-hundred-year-old toilet?"

"No, a *musical* toilet!" said Stink. "You put a coin in—"

"You have to pay to go to the toilet?" Judy asked. "That stinks."

"You go inside, and you're in this round room, and it's all white and clean – really, really clean – and it plays music!"

"I thought he'd never come out," Mum said.

“C’mon. We can quick hop the subway over to the Tea Party Ship,” said Dad.

“Finally!” said Judy.

“More old stuff? I declare NO FAIR!” Stink shouted.

Sugar and Spies

She, Judy Moody, declared independence from Stink. She ran up the planks ahead of him. She climbed aboard the *Beaver*, the Boston Tea Party Ship!

"Is this a real ship?" Stink asked.

"It's a real ship," said a guy wearing a wig and dressed like Paul Revere. "But it's not old, like the real *Beaver*. We built it to show what the Tea Party ship looked like."

"Finally! Something NOT old!" said Stink.

Judy climbed some ropes. So did Stink. She tried out a hammock. So did Stink. She went down the ladder into the dark cargo hold. So did Stink.

"Stink! How can I declare independence from you if you keep following me everywhere?"

Judy went back on deck. The Wig Guy was explaining about the men who wore disguises, sneaked aboard ship after dark and threw a million dollars worth of tea overboard.

"Who'd like to try throwing tea into Boston Harbour?"

Judy rushed to the front. Stink followed (of course!). They picked up bales tied with rope. Judy heaved a bale of tea over the side. "I won't drink tea! Taxes are NO FAIR!"

"Take that, King George!" said Stink as he tossed a bale off the ship.

"Who else wants to try?" Wig Guy pointed to a girl wearing bunny ears and carrying a bag that said BONJOUR BUNNY.

"C'mon, now. Wouldn't you like to give 'er the old heave-ho?"

"No," said the girl. "I quite like tea." She had a funny accent.

"From England, are you?" asked the man. The girl nodded.

TEA
H
TEA

"How exciting. This lass has come all the way from *across the pond*, as they say, just to see our ship!" The girl beamed.

"Glad to have you aboard, lassie!" Wig Guy shook her hand. "The Revolution was a long time ago. Let's be mates!"

The girl with the freckles and the funny voice was from England! Where they drank tea and had a queen. Judy had never met a real-live person from a whole other country before. Rare!

"I'm going to talk to her," Judy told Stink.

"You can't! She's a Redcoat! One of the Bad Guys!"

Judy looked around, but the Girl from

Across the Pond was nowhere in sight. Just then, Mum called for Judy and Stink to go to the gift shop.

Judy wandered up and down the aisles. Boxes of tea, bags of tea, tins of tea. Teapots and teacups and teaspoons. Stink followed her.

"Look! A tricorn hat!" She tried it on. "Stink, can I borrow some money? I want to get this hat."

"It's my money," said Stink. "From my allowance. Use your own."

"But I already spent mine at the Old North Church gift shop. On a Declaration of Independence and a *Paul Revere's Ride* flip book. I should get more allowance because I'm older than you. C'mon, Stink. You always have money."

"No way," said Stink.

"Redcoat!" Judy said.

"Yankee Doodle!" Stink said.

"Lobsterback!" said Judy.

"Chowder Head!" said Stink.

"Red Belly!" said Judy.

"Blue Belly!" said Stink.

"Kids! Keep it down," said Dad.

"Stink, stop following me around and stop getting me in trouble. Don't forget, I'm independent of you now." Judy walked away, past the drums and pennywhistles.

There she was! The tea drinker girl from England was not even looking at tea. She

CASHIER
JULIE KING
Bonjour Bunny

was looking at snow globes. Of Boston. Judy liked snow globes, too!

"Are you really a Red – I mean, from England?"

"Of course," said the girl. Her voice sounded snooty, as if the queen herself made the girl's bed.

"Does the queen make your bed?" asked Judy.

"WHAT?"

"Never mind. I was just wondering. What's your name?" Judy asked.

"Victoria. But you can call me Tori."

Stink popped up from behind a spinner rack. "Tory! Tories were the Bad Guys in the Revolution!" he said.

"Stink, stop spying on us!" said Judy.

She turned back to Tori. "Um ... what's that rabbit on your bag?" she blurted.

"It's Bonjour Bunny. I'm freaky for Bonjour Bunny! I have the backpack, jim-jams and sleeping bag. I even have my own Bonjour Bunny alarm clock! I just got the phone for my birthday. And the flannel, I mean washcloth, for my bathroom in our flat."

"Flat? You have a tyre in your house?"

"No, it's our apartment. Mum has her bathroom and I have mine."

PHONE! BATHROOM! WASHCLOTH! Judy's mum and dad would never let her have a phone. Or her own bathroom. At home, Judy had to use any old washcloth. Even ones with Stink cooties.

"I collect stuff, too," said Judy. "Mostly Barbie-doll heads and pizza tables. My newest collection is ABC gum. I stick it on the lamp in my room."

"ABC gum?" asked the girl.

"Already Been Chewed – I label each piece, like a rock collection."

"Fab!" said Tori. "I've never heard of that."

"And I collect pencils," said Judy. "And Band-Aids."

"Brilliant!" said Tori. "We call them plasters, not Band-Aids."

"Do you collect tea?" asked Judy.

"No. But I do collect sugar packets with pictures on them." Tori opened her purse. It was filled with sugar packets! She, Judy Moody, Collector of the World, had never even *thought* of collecting sugar packets.

"I have American presidents and flags of the world," said Tori. "Famous paintings. Hotel names ... boring! Famous women, too. See? Here's one of Susan B. Anthony."

"Do you have Amelia Bloomer? She gave a speech on Boston Common in her undies," said Judy.

"In her knickers?" asked Tori.

"Really they were bloomers. Some people call them pant-a-loons. Because they're *loons* if they think girls can't wear pants," said Judy.

"At least it wasn't in her nuddy pants,"

Tori whispered. "That means *bare naked*!" Judy and Tori cracked up.

"I did get some at the cafe with Ben Franklin sayings!" Tori added. "See?"

Judy read the sugar packets. "'Don't cry over spilled milk.' 'If your head is made of wax, don't stand out in the sun.'" She cracked up some more. "Brilliant!" said Judy. "My little brother will be so jealous!" She looked around. She didn't see Stink anywhere.

"The short one? Been spying on us? Maybe he's gone to the loo."

"The what?" Judy asked.

"You know." Tori pointed to the toilet.

"The loo! That's cuckoo!" Judy didn't see her mum and dad either. "Well, I'd better go and find my family," she said. "We're supposed to eat lunch at the snack bar."

"Me too! I'll go and fetch my mum."

"See you there," said Judy.

"Cheers!" said Tori. "Wait – what's your name?"

"Judy. Judy Moody."

"Brilliant!" said Tori.

In a Nark

Judy found Mum, Dad and Stink at the checkout. Dad was getting a ship-in-a-bottle kit to make a model of the *Beaver*. Mum was buying stuff to sew a cross-stitch pillow of the Paul Revere statue with the Old North Church in the background. Stink was holding a tin of Boston Harbour tea and waving a flag with a snake on it that said, DON'T TREAD ON ME.

Judy paid for her hat (with Stink's money), and they walked to the snack bar.

"You owe me four dollars and ninety-seven cents plus tax," said Stink.

"Tax! Mum! Dad! Stink's going all British on me. I need a raise in my allowance so I can pay him back."

"We'll talk about more allowance when we get home," said Mum.

"Time for lunch," said Dad. "I need a coffee."

"Not tea?" asked Mum.

"Just being loyal to my country," Dad said.

"Can I try coffee?" asked Judy. "I want to be loyal to my country, too."

"Dream on," said Dad.

"How about tea?"

"How about chocolate milk?" said Dad.

"The Boston Chocolate Milk Party. How UN-Revolutionary."

Judy ordered a Ben Franklin (cheese toastie with French fries). In the middle of bite three of her Ben Franklin, she said, "Hey, there's Tori!"

"Tori the Tory," said Stink.

Tori and her mum came over. While everybody met, Tori showed Judy all the new Bonjour Bunny stuff in her bag.

"You have all the luck!" said Judy. "I need more allowance. For sure and absolute positive."

"Mum gives me two pounds a week," said Tori.

"Star-spangled bananas!" said Judy. Tori got *pounds* of allowance! All Judy got was a few stinky ounces.

"C'mon," said Tori. "Let's collect more Ben Franklin sugar packets." While the grown-ups talked and Stink blew bubbles in his un-Revolutionary chocolate milk, Judy and Tori sat at an empty table and spread out all the sugar packets.

A penny saved is a penny earned.

Don't cry over spilled milk.

Fish and visitors stink after three days.

"Let's make up our own!" said Judy. She wrote on the backs of the packets:

A penny saved is never as much as Stink has.

Fish and little brothers stink after three days.

"Crikey! That's jolly good!" said Tori. She made one up, too:

Don't cry over spilled chocolate milk.

Judy taught Tori how to play Concentration with sugar packets. Tori showed Judy how to build a sugar-packet castle. When it was time to go, Judy did not want to leave her new friend.

"Mum? Dad? Can Tori come back to the hotel with us?" Judy asked.

"Or can Judy go swimming at our hotel with us?" Tori asked her mum.

"Can Tori come to Chinatown with us tonight?"

"Can Judy sleep over at our hotel? We

can sleep on the floor like we do in our flat at home."

Mum looked at Dad. Dad looked at Mum. "I don't think so, honey."

"AW! Why not?" asked Judy.

"We've only just met Tori," said Mum.

"Yes, that's right, girls," said Tori's mum.

"Please, Mum," said Tori. "Judy's so much fun."

"Judy and her family have got their own plans," said Tori's mum. "And we have tickets for the Duck Tour later this afternoon."

"Besides, we have to get an early start in the morning, Judy. It's back home to Virginia tomorrow," Dad said.

"Please-please-pretty-please with sugar packets on top?" Judy begged. "This is our one and only chance. We might never see each other again ever. Please? It would be brilliant!"

Mum shook her head no.

"Not even on account of the Revolution? I'm American and she's British and it's really good if we're friends. We could change history!"

"We said no, honey," Dad said.

"Well," said Tori's mum, "it's been lovely meeting you and your family, Judy. Hasn't it, Tori?"

"Crumb cakes!" said Tori. She hung her head. She kicked at a stone.

"Now, don't get in a nark," said Tori's mum.

"Who's going in an ark?" asked Stink.

"A nark," said Tori's mum. "It means a bad mood."

"Ohh. My sister has narks ALL the time," said Stink.

"Maybe when Tori gets back to London and we get home," said Mum, "you two can write to each other. Like pen pals!"

"That would be lovely," said Tori's mum. "Wouldn't it, Tori?" Tori didn't answer. "Well, we'd better be going," said her mother.

"Here, you can have these," Tori told Judy. "To remember me by." She gave Judy her Bonjour Bunny ears.

Judy gave Tori a whole packet of gum. "You can start your own ABC collection," said Judy.

Tori wrote down her address in London. Judy gave Tori her address in Virginia. "We can send each other sugar packets!" Tori whispered. "It'll be the bee's knees!"

Judy did not feel like the bee's knees.

She, Judy Moody, was in a nark. Not a good nark. A bad nark.

The Purse of Happiness

Judy was in a nark for four hundred and forty-four miles. She was in a nark all the way through Rhode Island, Connecticut, New York and Pennsylvania. (She slept through Maryland.) She was even in a nark through Home of the Presidents, Washington, DC.

Judy Moody was in a nark for seven hours and nineteen minutes. A Give-Me-Liberty nark.

"Mum! Judy won't play car games with me."

Stink wanted to count cows. Stink wanted to play the number plate game. Stink wanted to play Junior Scrabble.

"Judy," said Mum. "Play Scrabble with your brother."

"It's *baby* Scrabble!" said Judy. "I know. Let's play the silent game. Where you see how long you can go without talking."

"Hardee-har-har," said Stink.

"I win!" said Judy.

"Hey, you two," said Mum.

"It's her fault," said Stink.

"Judy, you're not still in a mood about Tori, are you?" asked Mum.

"You never let me do stuff," said Judy. "You should hear all the stuff Tori gets to do in England! She has tons of sleepovers. She even has her own phone. And her own bathroom! And she gets pounds of allowance. You think I'm still a baby or something."

"Or something," said Stink.

"Judy, if you want us to treat you like you're more grown-up, and if you want a raise in your allowance, then you'll have to show us that you can be more responsible."

"And not always get in a mood about everything," said Dad.

"I've never even had a sleepover before!" said Judy.

"Maybe when we get home, you can have a sleepover with Jessica Finch," said Mum.

"When cows read," said Judy. She, Judy Moody, was moving to England. She chewed two pieces of ABC gum, loud as a cow. She blew bubbles. *Pop! Pop! Pop-pop-pop!*

"She's still in a mood!" announced Stink.

In her mood journal, Judy made up nicknames for Stink all the rest of the way home.

Stinker
Stink-o-lator
Stink-o-rama
The Stinkster
Stink Bug
The Stink Man
Stink McFink
Stink-a-roni

@ @ @

When Judy got home, she dragged her tote bag upstairs to her room. *Thwump, thwump, thwump.* She dragged her backpack, her blanket, her pillow and her sock monkey. And her stuff from the gift shop. She shut the door and climbed up into her secret hideaway (her top bunk).

She, Judy Moody, was supposed to be writing her book report, as in not waiting till the very, very last minute. Instead, she declared freedom from homework.

Then she, Judy Moody, had an idea. A freedom idea. A John Hancock idea. A Declaration of Independence idea.

She did not even stop to call Rocky and tell him about the Boston Tea Party Ship and the Giant Milk Bottle that sold star-spangled bananas. She did not even stop to call Frank and tell him about Mother Goose's grave and the musical toilet.

That could wait till tomorrow.

But some things could not wait.

Judy gazed in awe at the copy of the Declaration of Independence she'd got in Boston. It was on old-timey brown paper with burned edges that looked like tea had been spilled on it. Judy squinted to try to read the fancy-schmancy handwriting.

When in the bones of human events ... blah, blah, blah ... we hold these truths ... more blah, blah ... alien rights ... Life, Liberty and the Purse of Happiness.

She, Judy Moody, would hereby, this day, make the Judy Moody Declaration of

Independence. With alien rights and her own Purse of Happiness and everything.

Judy pulled out the paper place mat she had saved from the Milk Street Cafe. The back was brown from chocolate-milk spills. Perfect! At last, Judy Moody knew what Ben Franklin meant when he said *Don't cry over spilled milk.*

The real Declaration of Independence had been written with a quill pen. Luckily, she, Judy Moody, just happened to have a genuine-and-for-real quill pen from the gift shop.

Look out, world! Judy mixed some water into the black powder that came with the pen, dipped the feather pen into the ink and wrote:

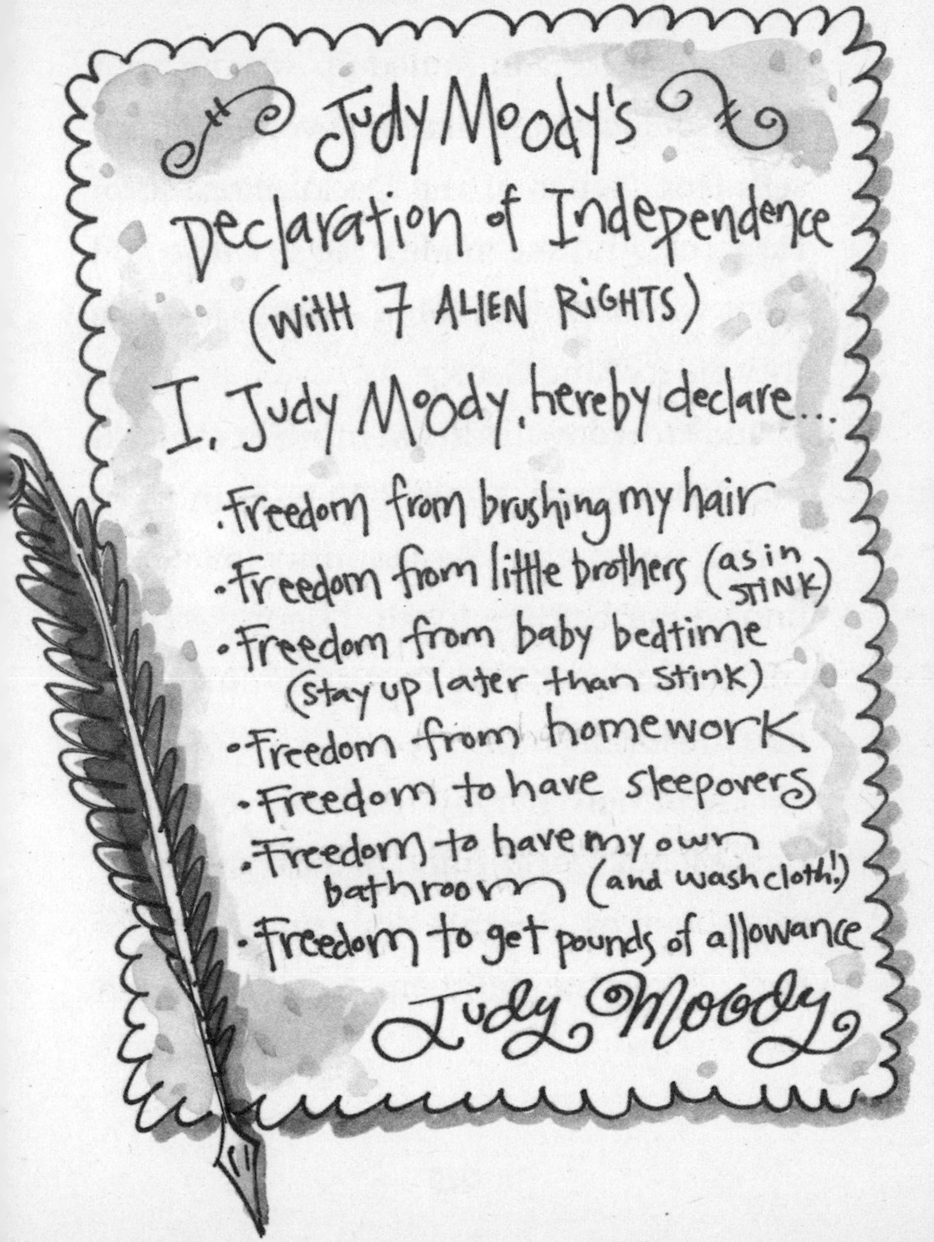
Judy Moody's
Declaration of Independence
(WITH 7 ALIEN RIGHTS)
I, Judy Moody, hereby declare...
• Freedom from brushing my hair
• Freedom from little brothers (as in STINK)
• Freedom from baby bedtime (stay up later than Stink)
• Freedom from homework
• Freedom to have sleepovers
• Freedom to have my own bathroom (and washcloth!)
• Freedom to get pounds of allowance
Judy Moody

She signed it in joined-up writing with fancy squiggles, just like Mr Revolution Himself, First Signer of the Declaration, John Hancock. And she made it big so Dad could see it without his reading glasses, just like they did for King George.

Judy ran downstairs wearing her tricorn hat. Where was Mouse? Judy found her curled up in the dirty-laundry pile. She jingled her cat like a bell. "Hear ye! Hear ye!" she called. Mum, Dad and Stink came into the family room.

"I will now hereby read my very own Judy Moody Declaration of Independence, made hereby on this day, the fourth of Judy. I hereby stand up for these alien rights – stuff like Life, Liberty and definitely the Purse of Happiness." Judy cleared her throat. "Did I *say* *hereby*?"

"Only ten hundred times," said Stink.

Judy read the list aloud, just like a town crier (not town crybaby). At the end, she took off her tricorn hat and said, "Give me liberty or give me death!"

"Very funny," said Dad.

"Very clever," said Mum.

"No way do you get to stay up later than me," said Stink.

"So you agree?" Judy asked Mum and Dad. "I should get all these freedoms? And a load more allowance?"

"We didn't say that," said Dad.

"We'll think it over, honey," said Mum.

"Think it over?" said Judy. Thinking it over was worse than maybe. Thinking it over meant only one thing – N-O.

Then Dad started talking like a sugar packet. "Freedom doesn't come without a price, you know," he told Judy.

"Dad's right," said Mum. "If you want more freedom, you're going to have to earn it – show us you can be more responsible."

Judy looked over her list. "Can I at least have Alien Right Number One? If I didn't have to brush my hair every day, I'd have more time to be responsible."

"Nice try," said Dad.

Parents! Mum and Dad were just like

King George, making up Bad Laws all the time.

"You guys always tell me it's good to stand up for stuff. Speak up for yourself and everything." Judy held up her Declaration. "That's what I just did. But I'm not even one teeny bit more free. That really stinks on ice!"

"Tell you what." Mum looked over the list. "You can have your own washcloth." Dad started to laugh but turned it into a cough.

"Tori has her own phone AND her own bathroom. And pounds of allowance. She can buy all the Bonjour Bunny stuff she wants, without even asking. And she drinks tea. And wakes herself up with her own alarm clock. And she has sleepovers in her flat that's not a tyre."

"We're not talking about Tori," said Mum. "We're talking about you."

Crumb cakes! She, Judy Moody, did not have any new freedoms at all. Not one single alien right from her list. All she had was a lousy washcloth.

"ROAR!" said Judy.

"If you don't want the washcloth, I'll take it," said Stink.

Huzzah!

Judy went to bed her same old un-free self. But the next morning, she decided Mum and Dad and the world would see a brand-new Judy Moody. A free and independent Judy. A more responsible Judy. Even on a school day.

Judy started by getting out of bed (without an alarm clock) before her mum had to shake her awake.

Next, she brushed her teeth without

complaining. Mum had set out a new blue washcloth – a plain old boring blue wash-cloth, but it was just for her. Judy wrote *Bonjour Bunny* on it, and made the capital *B*s into funny bunny ears.

Then Judy did something she had not done for three days. She brushed her hair (and put on her Bonjour Bunny headband from Tori). A responsible person did not have bird's-nest hair.

Then Judy did something she had not done for three weeks. She made her bed. A grown-up, independent person did not have a bed that looked like a garage sale.

On the bus, Judy told Rocky about the star-spangled bananas at the Giant Milk Bottle and the Sugar Packet Girl named Tori and about throwing tea off the Tea Party Ship. She could not wait to tell her teacher and her whole class.

"What are you going to tell your class about Boston?" she asked Stink.

"The musical toilet," said Stink. "What else?"

When Judy got to school, she told Mr Todd and the whole class all about Boston. "We went on the Freedom Trail and it was so NOT boring, and it's OK I missed my spelling test because I learned stuff there, too, like about Mr Ben Famous Franklin and Paul Revere and—"

"Judy! Take a breath!" said Mr Todd. "We're glad to have you back."

Judy showed them her *Paul Revere's Ride* flip book and explained all about tea and taxes to the class.

"My mum drinks tea and she's not a traitor," said Rocky.

"I went to Boston once to visit my grandpa," said Jessica Finch.

"Sounds like you had quite an educational trip, Judy," said Mr Todd. "Thanks for sharing with us. Maybe I'll read your book aloud in our reading circle today.

First, let's take out our maths facts from yesterday."

Judy multiplied 28 x 6, 7, 8, 9 and 10 until she thought her eyes would pop. At last, Mr Todd announced it was reading-circle time.

"Today I'll be reading a poem Judy brought to share with us from her trip to Boston, called *Paul Revere's Ride*. This poem tells a story."

"I saw his house and his real wallpaper and his false teeth and everything!" said Judy.

"This was my favourite poem when I was a boy," Mr Todd continued. "In school, we had to memorize it and recite it by heart.

It's by a man named Henry Wadsworth Longfellow. The poem is about three men and their famous midnight ride during the American Revolution. One of those men was Paul Revere."

Judy raised her hand. "And one was a doctor!" she told the class.

"Shh!" said Jessica Finch.

Mr Todd lowered his voice to a whisper. Class 3T got super quiet.

"'Listen, my children, and you shall hear
Of the midnight ride of Paul Revere…'"

The poem told all about how Paul Revere rode on horseback through the night to warn each farm and town that the British were coming.

Judy raised her hand again. "Mr Todd, Mr Todd! I saw Ye Olde Church where they hung the lanterns! For real! You know how it says, 'One if by land, two if by sea'? Paul Revere said to light one lantern if the British were sneaking in by land, two if they were coming across the water."

"Did that guy really ride his horse and do all that stuff?" asked Jessica Finch. "Because I never even heard about it the whole time I was in Boston."

"It's true," said Mr Todd. "Paul Revere warned two very important people, Sam Adams and John Hancock, to flee. But before he could warn everybody, he was stopped by the British and his horse was taken."

"But the doctor escaped and warned everybody!" said Judy.

"That's right," said Mr Todd. "You know, there's also a girl who had a famous ride just like Paul Revere. Her name was Sybil Ludington."

Star-spangled bananas! A Girl Paul Revere! Judy Moody could not believe her Bonjour Bunny ears.

"They don't often tell about her in the history books," said Mr Todd, "but we have a book about her in our classroom library."

"Huzzah!" said Judy Moody.

"Huh?" asked Frank.

"It's Revolutionary for YIPPEE!" Judy said.

The UN-Freedom Trail

She, Judy Moody, was the luckiest kid in Class 3T. Mr Todd let her take the Girl Paul Revere book home. Judy read it to Rocky on the bus. She read it to Mouse the cat. She read it to Jaws the Venus flytrap.

Sybil Ludington lived in New York, and her dad needed someone to ride a horse through the dark, scary forest to warn everybody that the British were burning down a nearby town. Sybil was brave and told her dad she could do it. She stayed up late past midnight and rode off into the dark all by herself. Sybil Ludington sure was grown-up and responsible. She showed tons of independence.

Judy would be just like Sybil Ludington. Responsible. Independent. All she had to do was prove it to Mum and Dad. There was only one problem.

She, Judy Moodington, did not have a horse.

And she would never in a million years be allowed to stay up past midnight.

Crumb cakes! She'd just have to be responsible right here in her very own house, 117 Croaker Road. Starting N-O-W.

Judy went from room to room all over the upstairs. She picked stuff up, put stuff away, hid stuff in the closet. Downstairs, she picked up one cat-hair fur ball, two giant lint balls, her basketball, Stink's soccer ball and Mouse's jingle ball.

Being responsible sure made a person hungry.

Judy stopped to eat some peanut butter out of the jar with a spoon (not her finger!). She stopped to feed Mouse (not peanut butter) and empty out the litter box (P.U!). She stopped to do some homework (without one single peanut-butter fingerprint!).

Mum and Dad were always bugging her to be nice to Stink, so she went up to his room to be nice. She looked on his desk. She looked under his bed.

"What are you looking for?" asked Stink.

"I'm looking for something nice to say," said Judy. "I like that ant farm poster on your wall."

"You gave it to me," said Stink.

"Well, um ... your hair looks good."

"Did you put something in my hair?" Stink shook his head. "Eeww, get it out!"

"Stink! Nothing's in your hair. Not even a spider."

Stink plucked at his hair like a dog with fleas.

"I said *not even*! I was just trying to be nice."

Judy never knew independent people had to be so nice. And so clean. But wouldn't Mum and Dad be surprised when they saw all the stuff she could do on her own? Without anybody telling her she had to. She, Judy Moody, would be Independent-with-a-capital-*I*. Just like Sybil Ludington. For sure and absolute positive.

Judy traced her feet onto red paper. *Snip, snip, snip*! She made a trail of red footprints all through the house. Not a messy, drop-your-stuff-everywhere trail. An independent, show-how-responsible-you-are trail. She even made signs for each stop along the way, just like the real Freedom Trail.

Now all she had to do was find Mum and Dad and Stink.

"The trail starts here," said Judy. She pointed to the sign in front of a wilted, half-dead plant: YE OLDE LIBERTY TREE.

"First I'll make a speech at Ye Olde Liberty Tree. Hear ye! Hear ye!" called Judy, jingling Mouse again. "Give me liberty or give me more allowance!" Mum and Dad laughed. Stink snorted.

"Listen, ye olde trail people. I'm Judy. I'll be your tour guide. Follow the red footprints to freedom!" Judy led her family from room to room.

On the dining room table, it said, JUDY MOODY DID HOMEWORK HERE.

"I do my homework there every day," said Stink. Judy gave him ye olde hairy eyeball.

On the kitchen floor, Judy pointed to a sign that said, JUDY MOODY FED MOUSE HERE.

"Isn't that one of your chores already?" asked Dad.

"Yes," said Judy. "But nobody had to remind me to do it."

She pointed to the kitchen table: JUDY MOODY ATE PEANUT BUTTER HERE.

"I don't get it," said Stink.

"I ate it with a spoon, not my fingers, and I didn't eat any in my room or get it on stuff," said Judy.

Judy Moody ate peanut Butter here
Judy Moody FED Mouse Here

Judy opened the door to the laundry room: JUDY MOODY PICKED UP LINT BALLS HERE. She opened the door to the downstairs bathroom: JUDY MOODY WASHED THE SOAP HERE.

"I hate the dope who thought up soap," Stink recited, cracking himself up. "I wish he'd eat it. I repeat it. Eat it."

Stink was not helping on the trail to freedom one bit. "Stink, stop saying stuff," said Judy.

"It's a free country," said Stink.

They followed the red footprints up the stairs to Judy's room. A sign on the bottom bunk said, JUDY MOODY MADE THE BED HERE. One on the top bunk said, PRIVATE! DON'T LOOK UP HERE.

"What are all those lumps up there?" asked Stink.

"Next stop, Stink's room," said the tour guide. His door had a sign taped to it: JUDY MOODY WAS NICE TO STINK HERE.

"Were not!" said Stink.

"Was too!" said Judy.

"Ha!" said Stink. "You told me I had a spider in my hair!"

"Last but not least, the big bathroom!" said Judy. JUDY MOODY PICKED UP THE P.U. TOWELS HERE.

"So what do you think?" Judy asked. "Wasn't I super-duper, Sybil-Ludington responsible?"

"This is great, honey. Everything looks

really good," said Dad. "You're starting to show us that you can be responsible and do things independently."

"It's nice when we don't have to tell you all the time," said Mum.

"So I can have more freedoms now? Like not brushing my hair all the time? And staying up later than Stink?"

"I want freedoms, too!" said Stink. "Chocolate milk for breakfast!"

"We're proud of you, Judy," Mum said. "But these are all things we want you to do anyway."

"You already get an allowance for doing these things," said Dad.

Tarnation! Judy was in a nark again. The narkiest.

The Freedom Trail was not free at all. The UN-Freedom Trail.

She, Judy Moody, picked up P.U. towels and washed soap and ate peanut-butter-not-with-her-fingers for nothing.

"It's just plain ye olde not fair!" she cried.

The Boston Tub Party

When Judy got home from school the next day, there was a mysterious package waiting for her.

"It has queens on it!" said Stink.

"It's from Tori!" Judy tore off the tape. "Sugar packets! For my collection!" There were clipper ships and castles, knights and queens. Even famous London stuff like Big Ben and the World's Largest Ferris Wheel, the London Eye.

"Rare!" said Judy. "Here's one in French. '*Je vois le chat.*' Stink, can you read it?"

Stink squinted at the sugar packet. "I think it says, 'Your head is toast'."

"Does not!" said Judy. "Give it!" She read the back. "It says, 'I see the cat'."

Judy found some that Tori had made herself, with funny British sayings like nuddy pants and stuff.

Amazed = gobsmacked
Throw up = pavement pizza
Crazy = barmy, off your trolley

"Can I have the pavement pizza one?" asked Stink.

"You're off your trolley, Stink."

"When was I *on* my trolley?" he asked.

Judy read the Bonjour Bunny postcard.

"There's a bunch of tea bags here, too. Real English tea, like at the Boston Tea Party," Judy said. "Tori's barmy if she thinks I'm even allowed to drink all this tea."

"Only traitors drink tea from England," said Stink.

"I'll be a traitor," said Mum. "I'd love to try some English tea." She selected one in shiny blue foil and headed for the kitchen.

Wait just a Yankee-Doodle minute! Judy had a not-so-barmy, off-your-trolley idea. She was gobsmacked that she hadn't thought of it before.

Since Mum and Dad would not let her have more freedoms, she would rise up and protest. Brilliant!

@ @ @

The next day at school, Judy passed notes to Rocky and Frank:

On Saturday, Rocky and Frank rang the Moodys' doorbell at exactly two minutes past twelve. Judy and Stink both ran for the door. Stink got there first. "It's not a Toad Pee Club meeting!" he blurted. "Judy lied. It's a *Tea Party* Club!"

"No way," said Frank.

"I'm not drinking any old tea with a bunch of dolls," said Rocky.

"Not that kind of tea party," said Judy, dragging them up to the bathroom. "C'mon. It'll be fun. Ben Franklin's honour!"

"I see tea bags," said Frank. "And a teapot."

"This is boring," said Rocky.

"Look! It's the talking teapot!" said

Stink. "From when Judy was little." He pressed a button.

"I'm a little teapot," the teapot sang, "short ... like ... Stink."

"Did it just say 'short like Stink'?" Frank asked. He cracked up.

"No – it said 'short and stout'," said Stink. "The batteries are running out!"

"Forget about the teapot," said Judy. "This is a *Boston* Tea Party." Judy explained about the real Boston Tea Party. "It's a protest! Right here. In the bathtub!"

"What's a protest?" asked Frank.

"You get to yell about stuff that's not fair," said Judy.

"Then I protest having a tea party," said Rocky.

"And you get to dump tea in the bath-tub," said Stink.

"The Boston *Tub* Party!" said Judy.

"The Wig Guy said everybody dressed up and painted their faces so nobody would know who they were," said Stink.

"Way cool," said Frank.

Stink got a bunch of funny hats from his room. "I call the tricorn hat!" said Rocky.

"I have face paints," said Judy.

Frank painted a not-cracked Liberty Bell on her cheek.

"Did you know they rang the Liberty Bell when they first read the Declaration of Independence?" Judy told Frank.

Stink got a moustache. Rocky got a beard. And Frank got a Frankenstein scar.

Judy filled the tub with hot water. "OK, everybody think about stuff that's not fair. Ready? Now, on the count of three, throw your tea into the tub. One, two … WAIT!"

"What's wrong?" asked Frank.

"It has to be dark. The real Tea Party was after dark." She turned out the big light, and the night-light flickered on.

"We can pretend it's the moon," said Rocky. "At midnight."

"THREE!" called Frank. He took the lid off the pot and dumped the tea into the tub. Rocky and Judy ripped open boxes of tea and tea-bag wrappers.

"Hey, let me!" said Stink. "You guys are hogging."

"Stink, you be on the lookout. Blink the light if you hear Dad coming. One if by stairs, two if by hallway."

Stink stood by the door. "You forgot to hoot and holler and yell not-fair stuff," said Stink.

Everybody started yelling and throwing tea bags into the bathtub.

"No more homework!" said Rocky.

"More allowance!" said Judy.

"More chocolate milk!" said Stink.

"No baby-sitting! No litter patrol!" said Frank.

Stink took off his shoes and socks, hopped right into the tub and started acting like a teapot. He made one arm into a handle and one into a spout.

TEA

"I'm a little teapot, short and stout," he sang. "When I get all steamed up, hear me shout, 'Give me chocolate milk or give me death!'" He sprayed water out of his mouth.

"Ooh, you spat on me," said Rocky.

"You're getting us all wet!" cried Frank.

Judy thought she heard footsteps on the stairs. "The British are coming! The British are coming!" she warned.

A voice, a deep voice, a *Dad* voice, said, "Hey, what's all the—"

"Abandon ship! Abandon ship!" Judy cried.

"What in the world is going on up here?" asked Dad, opening the bathroom door. "Sounds like an elephant in the bathtub." He turned on the lights.

Water dripped from the walls like a rainforest. The floor was flooded with giant brown puddles. Stink drip-drip-dripped like a short and stout wet mop.

The tub water was a brown sea of murky, ucky, yucky tea. Tea bags bobbed up and down on the tiny bathtub waves. The Boston Mud Party.

"Judy?" asked Dad. "Stink?"

Stink pointed to Judy. "It was her idea!"

"We were having a Boston Tea Party," said Judy.

"Judy," said Dad. "Just a few days ago, you were showing off this *clean* bathroom."

"But Dad! It's a protest! For more freedoms."

"A mess this size sure isn't going to get you more allowance … or your own bathroom."

"Pretend this is Boston Harbour. We were just making history come alive. Like homework."

"Sorry. This harbour's closed. Rocky, Frank, it's time for you boys to go home. Judy, no more friends over for one week. And you'd better get this mess cleaned up before Mum gets home. You too, Stink."

"But I don't even want independence!" said Stink. "Just more chocolate milk."

"The Patriots swept up after they threw tea in the harbour," Dad said.

No friends for one week! This was just like what the British did to the Americans – one of those Bad Laws they called the In-tol-er-able Acts. Dad was closing down the tub just like the Big Meanies closed down the harbour after the real Tea Party!

Judy felt like stamping her feet (the Stamp Act). She felt like throwing sugar packets (the Sugar Act). She felt like declaring independence *on the wall* (in permanent marker)!

But just like all the Bad Laws in the world did not stop the Patriots, the Clean-the-Bathroom-Again Law and No-Friends-for-One-Week Law would not stop her. And they would not, could not, put her in a nark. They were just bumps in the road on the Judy Moody March to Freedom.

She, Judy Moody, would live by a Not-Bad Law, the Law of the Sugar Packet: *If at first you don't succeed, try, try again.*

Sybil La-Dee-Da

When Judy got out of bed on Monday morning, she did not stamp one foot. She did not throw one sugar packet. Instead, she quietly-and-to-herself declared independence from brushing her teeth and taking a shower. She did not want to mess up the bathroom again. EVER.

Her book report from when she was in Boston was due today. A book report was NOT going to put her in a bad mood. Even if she had waited till the last minute. Judy decided right then and there to make this her best-ever book report. That's what a responsible person would do.

She dressed up in her pilgrim costume – the one Grandma Lou had made for Halloween. *Ye olde pilgrimme costoom* had an apron and made Judy look just like a girl from the American Revolution. Judy wore regular-not-loony pants underneath the skirt for bloomers. And she made thirteen curls in her hair – one for each of the thirteen colonies.

"Who are you? Heidi?" Stink asked at breakfast.

"None of your beeswax," said Judy.

"Are you a nurse?"

"N-O!" said Judy.

"Hey, I know. You're Priscilla Somebody! Like a pilgrim?"

"No, I'm Revolutionary. The Girl Paul Revere. For my book report today."

"Oh. So you're that Sybil La-Dee-Da?"

It sure was hard to declare independence from bad moods when Stink was around.

"Bye, Mum. Bye, Dad," Judy called on her way out the door.

"Hey, wait for me!" Stink yelled.

"Sorry! I'm riding my faster-than-lightning bike to the bus stop!" Judy yelled back. And she was off.

Right before the end of the school day, it was time for Judy's book report. She asked Frank Pearl to help her. They stood up in front of the class.

"Mr Todd? I have a different kind of book report. It's acted out. Like a play."

"Cool!" said Rocky.

"The book I read is called *Sybil: The Female Paul Revere,*" Judy told her class. "It's about the Girl Paul Revere. And this," she said, pointing to Frank, "is the Boy Paul Revere. Frank – I mean Paul – is helping me, Sybil Ludington."

Judy started with a poem: "'Listen, my children, and you shall hear / Of a girl who rode way further than Paul Revere.'"

P.R.

SYBIL: Hey, Paul Revere? Why are you so famous?

PAUL: Because, Sybil Ludington, I rode my horse all night. I warned everybody the British were coming.

SYBIL: I did, too. My horse is named Star. It was dark. I was scared. It rained all night. I was brave. It was muddy.

PAUL: It wasn't muddy when I rode.

SYBIL: Well, la-dee-da.

"No fair! It doesn't say that here!" said Frank.

"I just added it," said Judy. "Keep reading."

PAUL: I'm forty years old and I rode sixteen miles.

SYBIL: I'm only sixteen and I rode almost forty miles.

PAUL: I made it to Lexington to warn Sam Adams and John Hancock.

SYBIL: Hey, Paul? Weren't you caught by the British?

PAUL: At first I wasn't. Then I was.

SYBIL: Didn't Mr Todd say they took your horse?

PAUL: Yes.

SYBIL: Aha! So you got caught and didn't finish warning everybody. I, Sybil Ludington, DIDN'T get caught, and I warned everybody. I yelled, 'Stop the British. Mustard at Ludingtons!' All the British had to go back on their ships. Then everybody came to my house for hot dogs (with mustard). Even Mr George Famous Washington. The end.

"Did Sybil What's-Her-Face really eat hot dogs?" asked Jessica Finch.

"She ate mustard," said Judy. "Ketchup wasn't invented yet."

Mr Todd chuckled. "Actually, the word is *muster*, not *mustard*. When Sybil rode her horse to warn everybody, she called them to muster, which means to get together."

"The other parts were all true," said Judy. "I give this book five *reallys*. As in really, really, really, really, really good. It was so good, I stayed inside at break to read it. It was so good, I read it to my cat and my Venus flytrap!"

"Thank you, Judy," said Mr Todd. "Sounds like Sybil Ludington really inspired you."

"Everybody should know about the Girl Paul Revere. Most people have never heard of her, because for some barmy reason they forgot to put girls in history books. I wouldn't even know about her if you hadn't told me."

"Maybe some others will want to read the book now," said Mr Todd.

"Sybil Ludington should be in our social studies book for everybody to read about. Girls should get to be in history books, too, you know. Especially girls who did independent stuff, don't you think?"

"Yes, yes, I do," said Mr Todd.

"Girls rule!" all the girls shouted.

"Huzzah!" said Judy.

The Declaration of UN-Independence

On the bus ride home, Rocky told Judy how much he liked her book report. "When I first saw you looking like a pilgrim, I was sure it would be boring. But it was WAY not boring."

"Thanks," said Judy. "I hope I get a way good grade and it shows my Mum and Dad how grown-up and responsible I am."

"Just think," Rocky said, "how super scary it must have been when Sybil rode through the woods … and it was dark and robbers were all around."

"But she had to stop the British from burning down the whole town of Danbury!"

"Yeah. But if she got caught, the bad guys might think she was a spy!" Rocky said.

Judy and Rocky talked about Sybil all the way home.

When they got off the bus, Judy started walking, then said, "Oops, I almost forgot. I rode my bike to the bus stop today."

"OK. See ya!" called Rocky as he loped off towards his house. Judy unlocked her bike. Behind her, the doors of the bus hissed and closed, and the brakes squeaked as it pulled away from the kerb.

Wait ... something was not right.

Stink?

STINK!

Stink did not get off the bus! Stink had never NOT got off the bus before.

@ @ @

Judy could not think. She was sure she'd seen him get ON the bus. Should she yell for help? Race home and get Mum?

“HEY!” yelled Judy. “Mr Bus Driver! HEY!” she shouted. The bus was already driving off down the street.

WWBFD? What would Ben Franklin do? Go to bed early? Save a penny? Judy did not think sugar packet sayings could help her now.

There was only one thing to do. Chase the bus!

Mum would worry if she didn’t come right home, but there was no time to go and tell her. Not when her brother was being kidnapped by a runaway bus.

She, Judy Moody, had to get her brother back. No matter how stinky he was, he was still her brother.

Judy hitched up her pilgrim skirt and

hopped on her bike. She pedalled hard. She pedalled fast. She rode like the wind. She rode like Sybil on Star. She chased that bus down the street and around the corner and up the hill and down the hill.

Cars whizzed by. *Whoosh!* Dirt flew in her face. She swerved to miss a big hole in the road. What if she fell off her bike and broke her head?

Judy kept riding. She rang her bell. She yelled, "HEY! Mr Bus! My brother's on there. GIVE! ME! BACK! MY! BROTHER!"

The bus kept going.

A dog barked at her. What if a big meany dog got loose and chased her? What if she got bitten by a wild dog? A wild dog with RABIES?

Judy pedalled faster. Wind flapped her skirt and whipped her thirteen curls every which way. A big green dustcart screamed by, way too close. Judy's wheels wobbled. Her handlebars shook. The truck honked at her, *wooomp*, deep like a foghorn. Her heart pounded.

What if she got run over by a P.U. dust-cart?

She rode her bike all the way to Bacon Avenue. Traffic! Cars! Trucks! Red lights!

Then she saw it. The bus! The school bus, bright as a big cheese in the middle of the road. It had crossed the intersection and was heading up the hill on the other side of Third Street.

Mum and Dad would FREAK if she crossed the busy street in the middle of traffic by herself. But they might freak more if she came home late … without Stink!

WWSLD? What would Sybil Ludington do? Sybil would think for herself. Be independent. Be brave.

Judy hopped off and wheeled her bike to the crossing. She waited for the red man on the sign to change to the green man. "Hurry up!" Judy yelled at the light. "The bus is getting away!"

Finally, the light changed. She looked both ways, took a deep breath and crossed the street safely.

Judy hopped back on her bike and zoomed up the hill. *Puff, puff, puff.*

Judy huffed and puffed until she caught up with the bus. "Stink!" she shouted, cycling on the pavement, right alongside the bus. The bus driver looked over. Judy pointed to the back of the bus. "My brother!"

At last! The bus stopped to let some kids off. The door rattled open. "My little brother … *puff, puff* … is … *puff, puff* … on that bus!" Judy yelled.

Stink was already rushing up to the front of the bus. "I fell asleep!" he told Judy. "And then I woke up and you were gone and I didn't know where I was! I was so scared."

"It's OK," said Judy. "I chased you and I found you and you're safe now." Stink clutched her shirtsleeve and wouldn't let go.

"Thank you," she said to the driver. "Thanks for stopping. C'mon, Stinker. Let's go home."

When Judy and Stink got home – over an hour late – Mum was Mad-with-a-capital-*M*. "I thought I asked you to come straight home after school," Mum said. "You scared me half to death!" She said she was scared and worried sick, but she did not look sick. Just M-A-D.

She did not even give Judy a chance to explain. "Judy, you know better than this. Go to your room. Now!"

"Stink should go to his room, too. He's the one who fell asleep and—"

Mum's lips turned into a thin white line. "I don't want to hear it!" said Mum. She pointed upstairs.

Judy slunk up to her room, crawled into bed and got under her baby quilt. She, Judy Moody, Friend of Sybil in History, was in trouble again. Trouble with a capital *T*. Worse than the Boston Tub Party.

Grown-ups! They acted like they wanted you to be all independent, but as soon as you were, they went and changed their minds. Independence. HA! All it did was get her in trouble.

Maybe if Judy just declared UN-independence, everything would go back

to the way it was. At least she wouldn't have to clean up so much. And get run over by P.U. dustcarts while chasing runaway buses.

Judy tried to do her homework, but all the spelling words looked like scrambled eggs. She tried chewing gum for her ABC collection, but all it did was stick to her teeth. She tried starting a scrapbook of her trip to Boston, but even the Declaration of Independence looked sad.

To cheer herself up, Judy wrote a postcard to Tori:

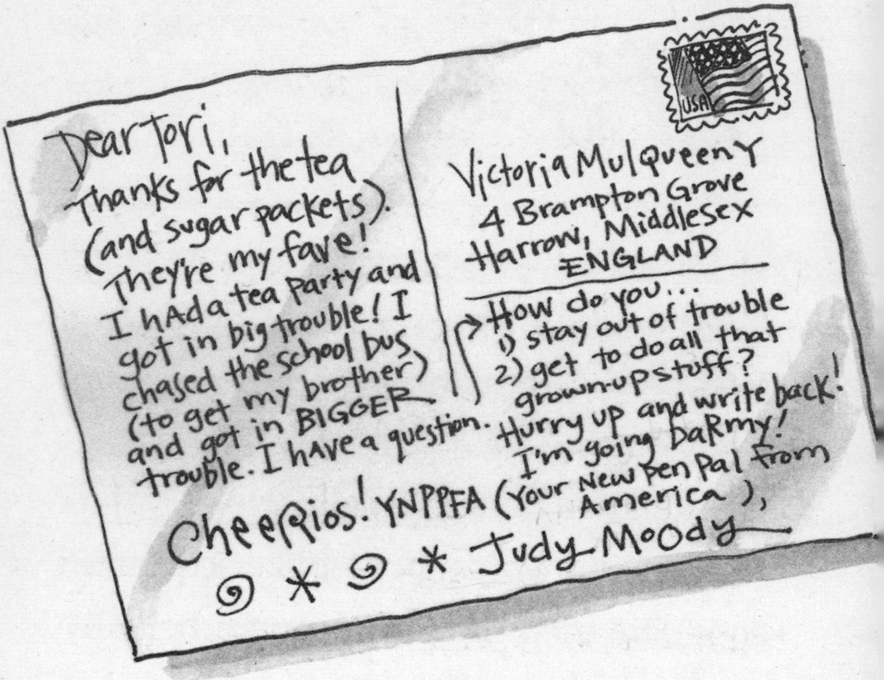

Judy tiptoed to the top of the stairs to see if she could hear anything. Mum was talking to Stink. Traitor! He was probably blaming the whole thing on her. Redcoat!

Judy climbed back up to her top bunk. "Here, Mouse," called Judy. At least her cat wasn't angry with her. At least her cat was not a traitor.

Mouse hid under the bottom bunk. "Here, Mousie, Mousie." Mouse still did not budge. Even her cat was declaring independence.

Judy's whole room was in a mood. For sure and absolute positive.

After about a hundred years, Stink rattled the doorknob. "Open up!"

"Go away, Stink," Judy told him.

"Open up, honey." That did not sound like Stink. That sounded like Mum. Nice Mum, not Will-You-Ever-Learn Mum.

"We just want to talk to you, Judy." That sounded like Dad. Kind Dad, not You-Are-in-Big-Trouble Dad.

"Am I in big trouble?" Judy asked the door. "Because if I am, then I declare UN-independence. I promise I will NOT make my bed or do my homework or be nice to Stink. And I will definitely NOT rescue him any more. EVER!"

"Judy, open the door so we can talk about this," said Dad.

Judy opened the door. Mum rushed to

hug her. Dad ruffled Judy's hair and kissed the top of her head.

"Stink told us what happened," said Dad. "That was a very brave thing you did."

"It was?"

"I'm sorry, honey," said Mum. "It gave me quite a scare when you two didn't come straight home, so I didn't even stop to listen. You had a hard choice to make and you really used some good, independent thinking."

"I did?"

"You sure did," said Dad.

"I was scared, too," said Judy. "I thought a big meany dog might bite me or a

dustcart might run me over or I'd fall and break my head or something. I just kept thinking about Sybil Ludington and how she was scared, too."

"We're very proud of you, Sybil," Dad said. "I mean Judy."

"Proud enough to give me more allowance and stuff?"

"Dad and I will talk things over," said Mum. "Maybe you *are* ready for a little more independence."

She, Judy Moodington, was not in big-or-little-*T* trouble. And she showed independent thinking. Just like Sybil Ludington.

Star-spangled bananas!

Yankee Doodle Dandy

After all the excitement, Judy was feeling much too independent to do homework. She got out her Judy Moody Declaration of Independence. This was going straight into her scrapbook.

Judy climbed up to her top bunk. She spread out all the stuff from her trip to Boston. In her scrapbook, she pasted, taped, glue-sticked or Band-Aided all her souvenirs from Boston.

Mother Goose
J.M.
Mother Goose died here
TEA
BOSTON
by J.M.
Amelia Bloomer Stood Her
BOSTON
DUCK TOUR

BOSTON CHILDREN'S MUSEUM
ADMIT ONE
BEN FRANKLIN
by J.M.
Stink's country pooed on him here
Stink acted like a baby here.
THE PAUL REVERE HOUSE
BOSTON, MASSACHUSETTS
BEAN TOWN
Paul Revere made false teeth and rang bells here (for real!)

Last but not least, she turned the page and glued sugar packets with Ben Franklin sayings onto the page. And she made up a new one:

If at first your brother falls asleep on the bus, ride, ride like Sybil and chase after him.

The next day, the story of the not-so-midnight ride of Judy Moody was all over Virginia Dare School.

Listen, my children, and you shall hear
How Judy Moody rode like Sybil and
Paul Revere.

Every time Stink told the story, it got a little wilder. Some heard she was chased by wild wolves. Some heard she was kidnapped by a dustcart. Some heard she fell and broke her leg but kept on riding.

Stink even made Judy a gold medal with a blue ribbon.

@ @ @

After dinner that night, Judy climbed up to her top bunk to glue the ribbon into her scrapbook.

The scrapbook was not there! As in G-O-N-E, gone!

She looked under her reading pillow. She looked under lumps of covers and heaps of stuffed animals. She looked under Mouse.

Judy looked all around her room. The

scrapbook was missing. The scrapbook was stolen! By Number One Scrapbook Thief, right here in the Moody house.

"Stink!" Judy ran into his room. "I did not say you could take my scrapbook. Give it!"

"I didn't take your scrapbook," said Stink.

"After I saved your life and everything!" said Judy. "Robber! Stealer! Scrapbook-napper!"

"Am not! I swear on Toady's life I didn't take it."

"If you didn't take it, and I didn't lose it, that leaves Mouse. And Mouse can't read!"

"Maybe Mum and Dad took it," Stink said. "Let's go and ask."

"Let's go and *spy*," said Judy.

Judy and Stink tiptoed down the stairs without too many creaks. They slid across the floor without too many squeaks. They slunk past the living-room, past the kitchen, to Mum's office.

"Stink, you hold the torch. I'll look around." She pawed through the rubbish. She searched on top of the filing cabinet and in the bookshelves.

"Uh-oh!" Stink said. "Check it out!" A message was flashing across Mum's computer screen. It said:

JUDY AND STINK,
IF YOU ARE READING THIS,
I KNOW YOU'RE IN HERE.
READ THIS NOTE:
XLOW UVVG ZIV MLG HDVVG.

"How can we read it? It's in Russian," Stink said, shining the light on the screen.

"It's not Russian," said Judy. "It's secret code. SPY code. It looks just like Dr Church's secret code in Dad's Freedom Trail book from Boston. Rare!"

"The spy guy? Sweet! We can be code busters, just like him."

"Yep." Judy ran and got her book. She looked it up in the back. "The code is A=Z, B=Y, and C=X. All you have to do is use the alphabet backwards."

They looked at the letters again: XLOW UVVG ZIV MLG HDVVG. Judy worked it out. "COLD FEET ARE NOT SWEET. Hmm. It's some sort of clue. Not sweet ... not sweet."

"How about the cookie jar?" Stink asked.

"It says NOT sweet, Stink."

"How about socks? Socks aren't sweet. And they help cold feet."

"Brilliant!" Judy and Stink dashed upstairs, where Judy rummaged through her sock drawer. Sure enough, there was another clue sticking out of her Screamin' Mimi's ice-cream socks.

"It's like a treasure hunt." She opened the note and it read: QFWB GRNVH GDL, YLGS ZIV BLF. She took out her pencil and worked it out in her notebook. "This one says, JUDY TIMES TWO, BOTH ARE YOU."

They thought about it for a long time. They were both stumped. Then Judy got a brainstorm! "There's only one me," said Judy.

"You can say that again," said Stink.

"Unless … I look in a mirror!" Judy and Stink raced for the bathroom. On the bathroom mirror, a message was written in soap crayons: Z SLFHV ULI NLFHV

Stink helped Judy work out the code. "A HOUSE FOR MOUSE!" yelled Judy.

"That doesn't make sense," said Stink.

"Think," said Judy. "What else could be a house for Mouse?"

"Under your bed?" asked Stink. "Or your top bunk?"

"I looked there," said Judy. "Wait! I got it! Where is Mouse whenever we can't find her?"

"The dirty-laundry basket!" said Stink. He ran downstairs after his sister. Judy raced over to the pile of laundry on the washing machine and dug around. "Found it!" she said, holding up her scrapbook.

They flipped through pages of pictures and pebbles, pressed leaves and pencil rubbings, tea bags and sugar packets and Band-Aids, her Declaration of Independence, the postcard from Tori.

She flipped to the last page. She, Judy Moody, was gobsmacked! Glued to the page was a fancy certificate on old-timey paper that looked like parchment.

SUDS
BOSTON

Hear ye! Hear ye! Judy Moody has hereby . . .

Made her bed every day
Brushed her hair (almost) every day
Done her homework without being asked
Been nice to Stink
Inspired others with her bravery and
courage on her famous ride

. . . which demonstrates independent thinking.
We, the undersigned (Mum and Dad), hereby
grant Judy Moody a 25¢ raise in her allowance,
effective now.
Signed,
Kate Betsy-Ross Moody (aka Mum)
Richard John-Hancock Moody (aka Dad)

Taped to the same page was a shiny new quarter.

"Holy macaroni!" said Judy. "Look! A Maine quarter with a lighthouse! Now I have liberty AND the purse of happiness."

"And with more allowance, you can pay me back a lot faster!" said Stink.

"Wait till I write to Tori and tell her. My Declaration of Independence really worked!"

"Except for the getting your own bathroom thing."

Judy Moody hugged her scrapbook, then Stink. She found Mum and Dad and hugged them, too. She even kissed Mouse on her wet pink nose.

"Independence doesn't end here," said Mum. "We're going to expect you to keep being responsible."

"And, of course, you still always have to do your homework," Dad told her.

"And be nice to me!" said Stink.

"Maybe I could also stay up a teeny-weeny bit late? Just for tonight?" asked Judy. "On account of how independent I am now and how I'm not going to be treated like a baby any more and stuff."

"Fifteen minutes," said Dad.

"And just for tonight," said Mum.

Fifteen whole minutes!

"No fair!" said Stink. "Then I'm declaring independence from brushing my teeth! Give me liberty or give me bad breath!"

"One independent kid is enough for now," said Mum. Dad laughed.

That night, in those fifteen minutes, Judy

ate a snack of grapes and goldfish (the crackers!). She brushed her teeth with red, white and blue toothpaste and washed her face with her very own (Bonjour Bunny) washcloth. She read a whole chapter of her *Ramona the Brave* library book. After only twelve and a half minutes, she couldn't even stay awake any more. She climbed the ladder to her top bunk.

"Lights out!" said Mum. "Goodnight, sweetie." Dad blew her a kiss.

After Mum and Dad pulled the door almost-shut, Judy lay on her top bunk and gazed up at the night-sky ceiling full of glow-in-the-dark stars.

Star-spangled bananas! She, Judy Moody,

was Independent-with-a-capital-*I*. As independent as Ben Franklin. John Hancock. Paul Revere. As independent as Sybil Ludington on her midnight ride.

Being independent was brilliant! The bee's knees. And staying up late was Yankee Doodle Dandy.

Judy was getting sleepy. So sleepy. But just before she drifted off, she took out her torch pen and wrote something on the wall, in permanent marker, right next to her pillow:

JUDY MOODY SLEPT HERE.

Judy Moody
Slept Here

JUDY MOODY SAVES THE WORLD!

Where would the world be
without Judy Moody?

Her class is learning about the environment, and Judy is startled to learn about the destruction of the rainforest and the endangered species in her own back yard – not to mention her own family's crummy recycling habits. So, never one to take things lying down, Judy Moody gets on the case!

JUDY MOODY PREDICTS THE FUTURE

Judy Moody has a mood for every occasion,
and now she has a mood ring to prove it!

Judy's mood ring has Extra Special Powers which have put Judy in a predicting mood, and her outrageous predictions have everyone wondering if she really is psychic. According to "Madame M" (for Moody), the Toad Pee Club's long-lost mascot will reappear, Judy will earn a coveted tricorn-hat sticker for getting 110% in her spelling test, and love may be the real reason behind her teacher's new glasses!

Will Judy's latest adventures put you in a very Judy Moody mood? The signs point to yes.

DOCTOR JUDY MOODY

Judy Moody's in a medical mood!

Judy has got the Moody Monday blues – until she gets to school and finds out that her new class project is on the Amazing Human Body. That means skeletons and skulls, a trip to the hospital to see a real-life doctor, and a cloning experiment that could just create some double trouble for Judy and her friends!